The Dominant Dollar

Will Lillibridge

Illustrated by Lester Ralph

By the Same Author

BEN BLAIR. THE STORY OF A PLAINSMAN.

With frontispiece in full color by Maynard
Dixon. *Seventh edition, 60th thousand.*

*** Besides the wide success of "Ben Blair"
in this country the book appeared in a large edition
in London and also in Australia.

"Most of all because I love you"

The
Dominant Dollar
By WILL LILLIBRIDGE

AUTHOR OF
"Ben Blair," "The Dissolving Circle," "The Quest
Eternal," "Where the Trail Divides," Etc.

WITH FOUR ILLUSTRATIONS
BY LESTER RALPH

September 11, 1909

CONTENTS

BOOK I

BOOK II

Illustrations

"Most of all because I love you"

"I'm tired of reading about life and hearing about life. I want to live it"

"Steve!" The girl was on her feet. "I never dreamed, never—You poor boy!"

"You mean to suggest that Elice," he began, "that Elice—You dare to suggest that to me?"

BOOK I

CHAPTER I

A PROPHECY

"You're cold-blooded as a fish, Roberts, colder. You're—There is no adequate simile."

The man addressed said nothing.

"You degrade every consideration in life, emotional and other, to a dollar-and-cents basis. Sentiment, ambition, common judgment of right and wrong, all gravitate to the same level. You have a single standard of measurement that you apply to all alike, which alike condemns or justifies. Summer and Winter, morning, noon, and night—it's the same. Your little yardstick is always in evidence, measuring, measuring—You, confound you, drive me to distraction with your eternal 'does it pay.'"

Still the other man said nothing.

"I know," apologetically, "I'm rubbing it in pretty hard, Darley, but I can't help it. You exasperate me beyond my boiling point at times and I simply can't avoid bubbling over. I believe if by any possibility you were ever to have a romance in your life, and it came on slowly enough so you could analyze a bit in advance, you'd still get out your tape line and tally up to the old mark: would it pay!"

This time the other smiled, a smile of tolerant amusement.

"And why shouldn't I? Being merely the fish you suggest, it seems to me that that's the one time in a human being's life when, more than another, deliberation is in order. The wider the creek the longer the wise man will linger on the margin to estimate the temperature of the current in event of failure to reach the opposite bank. Inadvertently, Armstrong, you pass me a compliment. Merely as an observer, marriage looks to me like the longest leap a sane man will ever attempt."

"I expected you'd say that," shortly, — "predicted it."

"You give me credit for being consistent, then, at least."

"Yes, you're consistent all right."

"Thanks. That's the first kind word I've heard in a long time."

The other made a wry face.

"Don't thank me," he excepted. "I'm not at all sure I meant the admission to be complimentary; in fact I hardly think I did. I was hoping for once I'd find you napping, without your measuring stick. In other words—find you—human."

"And now you're convinced the case is hopeless?"

"Convinced, yes, if I thought you were serious."

Roberts laughed, a big-chested, tolerant laugh.

"Seems to me you ought to realize by this time that I am serious, Armstrong. You've known me long enough. Do you still fancy I've been posing these last five years you've known me?"

"No; you never pose, Darley. This is a compliment, I think; moreover, it's the reason most of all why I like you." He laughed in turn, unconsciously removing the sting from the observation following. "I can't see any other possible excuse for our being friends. We're as different as night is from day."

The criticism was not new, and Roberts said nothing.

"I wonder now and then, at times like this," remarked Armstrong, "how long we will stick together. It's been five years, as you say. I wonder if it'll be another five."

The smile vanished from Darley Roberts' eyes, leaving them shrewd and gray.

"I wonder," he repeated.

"It'll come some time, the break. It's inevitable. We're fundamentally too different to avoid a clash."

"You think so?"

"I know so. It's written."

"And when we do?"

"We'll hate each other—as much as we like each other now. That, too, is written."

Again Roberts laughed. A listener would have read self-confidence therein.

"If that's the case, wouldn't it be wiser for us to separate in advance and avoid the horrors of civil war? I'll move out and leave you in peaceful possession of our cave if you wish."

"No; I don't want you to. I need you. That's another compliment. You hold me down to earth. You're a helpful influence, Darley, providing one knows you and takes you with allowance."

The comment was whimsical, but beneath was a deeper, more tacit admission which both men understood, that drowned the surface banter of the words.

"I think again, sometimes," drifted on Armstrong, "that if the powers which are could only put us both in a pot as I put things together down in the laboratory, and melt us good and shake us up, so, until we were all mixed into one, it would make a better product than either of us as we are now."

"Perhaps," equivocally.

"But that's the curse of it. The thing can't be done. The Lord put us here, you you, and me me, and we've got to stick it out to the end."

"And become enemies in the course of events."

"Yes," quickly, "but let's not think about it. It'll come soon enough; and meantime—" The sentence halted while with unconscious skill Armstrong rolled a cigarette—"and meantime," he repeated as he scratched a match and waited for the sulphur to burn free, "I want to use you." Again the sentence halted while he blew a cloud of smoke: "I had another offer to-day."

Following the other's example, Roberts lit a cigar, big and black, and sat puffing in judicial expectancy.

"It's what you'd call a darned good offer," explained Armstrong: "position as chemist to the Graham Specialty Company, who are building the factory over on the East side—perfumes and toilet preparations and that sort of thing."

"Yes."

"Graham himself came to see me. As a matter of fact he's the whole company. He labored with me for two hours. I had to manufacture an engagement out of whole cloth to get away."

"And you decided—"

"I didn't decide. I took the matter under advisement."

"Which means that you did decide after all."

Armstrong grimaced in a mannerism all his own, an action that ended in an all-expressive shrug. "I suppose so," he admitted reluctantly.

"I hardly see where I can be of service then," commented the other. "If you were ten years younger and a minor and I your guardian—"

"You might point out with your yardstick how many kinds of an idiot I am and stir me up."

His companion smiled; as suddenly the look passed.

"I'd do so cheerfully if it would do any good. As it is—" The sentence ended in comprehensive silence. "What, by the way, did Graham offer?"

"Five thousand dollars a year, and if I made good an interest later in the business. He said four thousand dollars to begin with and gradually crawled up."

"You're getting now from the University—"

"Twelve hundred."

"With ultimate possibilities,—I emphasize possibilities—"

"I'll be dean of the department some day if I stick."

"With a salary of two thousand a year."

Armstrong nodded.

"And that's the end, the top round of the ladder if you were to remain until you were fifty and were displaced eventually without a pension."

"Yes; that's the biggest plum on the university tree. It can't grow anything larger."

In his place Darley Roberts dropped back as though he had nothing to say. Involuntarily, with a nervous impatience distinctive of him, his fingers tapped twice on the edge of the chair; then, aroused to attention, the hand lay still.

"Well?" commented Armstrong at length.

Roberts merely looked at him, not humorously nor with intent to tantalize, but with unconscious analysis written large upon his face.

"Well?" repeated Armstrong, "I'm waiting. The floor is yours."

"I was merely wondering," slowly, "how it would seem to be a person like you. I can't understand."

"No, you can't, Darley. As I said a moment ago, we're different as day is from night."

"I was wondering another thing, too, Armstrong. Do you want to know what it was?"

"Yes; I know in advance I'll not have to blush at a compliment."

"I don't know about that. I'm not the judge. I merely anticipated in fancy the time when you will wake up. You will some day. It's inevitable. To borrow your phrase, 'it's written.'"

"You think so?" The accompanying smile was appreciative.

"I know so. It's life we're living, not fiction."

"And when I do—pardon me—come out of it?" The questioner was still smiling.

"That's what I was speculating on." Again the impatient fingers tapped on the chair, and again halted at their own alarm. "You'll either be a genius and blossom in a day, or be a dead failure and go to the devil by the shortest route."

"You think there's no possible middle trail?"

"Not for you. You're not built that way."

The prediction was spoken with finality—too much finality to be taken humorously. Responsively, bit by bit, the smile left Armstrong's face.

"I won't attempt to answer that, Darley, or to defend myself. To come back to the point, you think I'm a fool not to accept Graham's offer?"

As before, his companion shrugged unconsciously. That was all.

"Does it occur to you that I might possibly have a reason—one that, while it wouldn't show up well under your tape line, to me seems adequate?"

"I'm not immune to reason."

"You'd like to have me put it in words?"

"Yes, if you wish."

"Well, then, first of all, I've spent ten years working up to where I am now. I've been through the mill from laboratory handy-man to assistant demonstrator, from that to demonstrator, up again to quiz-master, to substitute-lecturer, until now I'm at the head of my department. That looks small to you, I know; but to me it means a lot. Two hundred men, bright fellows too, fill up the amphitheatre every day and listen to me for an hour. They respect me, have confidence in my ability—and I try to merit it. That means I must study and keep up with the procession in my line. It's an incentive that a man can't have any other way, a practical necessity. That's the first reason. On the other hand, if I went to work for Graham I'd be dubbing around in a back room laboratory all by myself and doing what he wanted done whether it was interesting in the least or not."

"In other words," commented Roberts, "you'd be down to bed rock with the two hundred admirers removed from the bed."

"I suppose so—looking at it that way."

"All right. Go on."

"The second reason is that my employment as full professor gives me an established position—call it social position if you wish—here in the University that I couldn't possibly get in any other way. They realize what it means to hold the place, and give me credit for it. We're all human and it's pleasant to be appreciated. If I went to work in a factory I'd be an alien—outside the circle—and I'd stay there."

"There are eighty million people in the United States," commented Roberts, drily. "By stretching, your circle would probably take in two thousand of that number."

"I know it's limited; but there's an old saying that it's better to be a big toad in a small puddle than a small toad in a large pond."

"I recall there's an adage to that effect."

"Lastly, there's another reason, the biggest of all. As it is now the State employs me to deliver a certain number of lectures a semester. I do this; and the rest of the time is mine. In it I can do what I please. If

I accepted a position in a private enterprise it would be different. I should sell my time outright—and be compelled to deliver it all. I shouldn't have an hour I could call my own except at night, and the chances are I shouldn't have enough energy left for anything else when night came. You know what I'm trying to do—that I'm trying to work up a name as a writer. I'd have to give up that ambition entirely. I simply can't or won't do that yet."

"You've been keeping up this—fight you mention for ten years now, you told me once. Is anything definite in sight?"

"No; not exactly definite; but Rome wasn't built in a day. I'm willing to wait."

"And meantime you're getting older steadily."

"I repeat I'm willing to wait—and trust a little."

Tap, tap went the impatient fingers again.

"Something's bound to drop in time if one is only patient."

Roberts looked up quickly, the gray eyes keen, the tapping fingers stilled.

"Something has dropped, my friend, and you don't recognize it."

"The tape line again. The eternal tape line! It's pure waste of energy, Darley, to attempt to make you understand. As I said before, you're fundamentally incapable."

"Perhaps," evenly. "But for your sake I've listened and tried. At least give me credit for that." Of a sudden he glanced up keenly. "By the way, you're not going out this evening?"

"No, Elice is out of town." Armstrong caught himself. "I suppose that is what you meant."

For a moment before he answered Roberts busied himself with a stray flake of ash on his sleeve.

"Yes, in a way," he said. "I was going to suggest that you tell her what you told me before you said 'no' to Graham."

"It's unnecessary." The tone was a trifle stiff. "She at least understands me."

The other man made no comment.

"You're not going out either this evening, Darley?" returned Armstrong.

"No; I'm scheduled for bed early to-night. I've had a strenuous day, and to-morrow will be another."

It was already late of a rainy May evening, the room was getting dim, and silently Armstrong turned on the electric light. Following, in equal silence, his companion watching him the while understandingly, he lit a pipe. Stephen Armstrong seldom descended to a pipe, and when he did so the meaning of the action to one who knew him well was lucid. It meant confidence. Back in his seat he puffed hard for a half minute; then blew at the smoke above his head.

"Was that mere chance that made you suggest—Elice in connection with that offer of Graham's," he asked, at last; "or did you mean more than the question seemed to imply, Darley?"

Again for an appreciable space there was silence.

"I seldom do things by chance, Armstrong. To use your own simile, I'm too much of a fish. I don't want to seem to interfere with your personal affairs, however. I beg your pardon if you wish."

"But I don't wish you to do so," shortly. "You know that. Besides there's nothing to conceal so far as I'm concerned. Just what did you mean to suggest?"

Again the other hesitated, with a reluctance that was not simulated. Darley Roberts simulated nothing.

"If you really wish to know," he complied at last, "I think you ought to tell, her—without coloring the matter by your own point of view in the least. She should be as much interested as you yourself."

"She is. Take that for granted."

Roberts waited.

"I know, though, so certainly what she would say that it seems a bit superfluous."

Still Roberts waited.

"As I said before, she understands me and I understand her. Some things don't require language to express. They come by intuition."

And still Roberts waited.

"If it were you, now, and there were any possibility of a yardstick it would be different; but as it is—"

"Miss Gleason then, Mrs. Armstrong to be, doesn't care in the least to see you come on financially, is completely satisfied with things as they are?"

It was Armstrong's turn to be silent.

"You've been engaged now three years. You're thirty years old and Miss Gleason is—"

"Twenty-five in August."

"She is wholly contented to let the engagement run on indefinitely, knowing that your income is barely enough for one to live on and not at all adequate for two?"

The other stiffened involuntarily; but he said nothing.

"I beg your pardon the second time, Armstrong, if you wish; but remember, please, I'm doing this by request."

"I know, Darley. I'm not an absolute cad, and I'm glad you are frank. Doubtless from your point of view I'm a visionary ass. But I don't see where any one suffers on that account except myself."

"Don't see where any one suffers save yourself! Don't see—! You can't be serious, man!"

Armstrong had ceased smoking. The pipe lay idle in his fingers.

"No. Come out into the clearing and put it in plain English. Just what do you mean?"

"Since you insist, I mean just this, Armstrong—and if you'll think a moment you'll realize for yourself it's true: you can't drift on forever the way you're doing now. If you weren't engaged it would be different; but you are engaged. Such being the case it implies a responsibility and a big one. To dangle so is unjust to the girl. Let this apply in the abstract. It's damnably unjust!"

"You think that I—"

"I don't think at all, I know. We can theorize and moon and drift about in the clouds all we please; but when eventually our pipe goes out and we come down to earth this thing of marriage is practical. It's give and take, with a whole lot to give. I haven't been practising law and dealing with marital difficulties, to say nothing of divorces, without getting a few inside facts. Marriages are made in Heaven, perhaps, but married life is lived right here on earth; and the butcher and the rest play leading parts. I recognize I'm leading the procession a bit now, Armstrong; but as I said before, you can't dangle much longer if you're an honorable man; and then what I've said is right in line. If you'll take a word of advice that's intended right, even if it seems patronizing, you'll wake up right now and begin to steer straight for the flag-pole. If you keep on floundering aimlessly and waiting for an act of Providence you'll come to grief as surely as to-morrow is coming, old man."

"And by steering straight you mean to save money. To get my eye on a dollar, leave everything else, and chase it until it drops from fatigue."

"I mean get power; and dollars are the tangible evidence and manifestation of power. They are the only medium that passes current in any country any day in the year."

Armstrong smiled, a smile that was not pleasant to see.

"You'd have me give up my literary aspirations then, let them die a-borning as it were—"

"I didn't say that. So far as I can see you can keep on just the same. There are twenty-four hours in every day. But make that phase secondary. I don't discount writers in the least or their work; but with the world as it is the main chance doesn't lie that way—and it's the main chance we're all after. Fish or no fish, I tell you some time you'll find this out for yourself. To get the most out of life a man must be in the position to pass current wherever he may be. In the millennium the standard may be different—I for one sincerely hope it will be; but in the twentieth century dollars are the key that unlocks everything. Without them you're as helpless as a South Sea islander in a metropolitan street. You're at the mercy of every human being that wants to give you a kick; and the majority will give it to you if they see you are defenceless."

Armstrong was still smiling, the same being a smile not pleasant to see.

"Now that I've got you going," he commented, "I've a curiosity to have you keep on. You're certainly stirring with a vengeance to-night, Darley."

"And accomplishing nothing. Strange as it may seem to you, I'm serious."

"I don't doubt it, old man." Of a sudden the smile had passed. "I can't adjust my point of view to yours at all. If I thought dollars were the end of existence I'd quit the game now. If the world has come to this—"

"The world hasn't come to it and never will. You simply can't or won't see the point. I repeat, that of themselves they're nothing, but they're the means to everything. Get your competency first, your balance-wheel, your independence, your established base of supplies; then plan your campaign. The world is big, infinitely big, to the human being who can command. It's a little mud ball to the other who has to dance whenever some one else whistles."

"And how about happiness, the thing we're all after?"

"It isn't happiness, but it's the means to it. There can be no happiness without independence."

"Even marital happiness?"

"That most of all. I tell you the lack of a sufficient income is the rock on which most married people go to pieces. It isn't the only one, but it's the most frequent. I've seen and I know."

"You'd drive our old friend Cupid out of business, Darley. You don't give him an inch of ground to stand on."

"On the contrary, I keep him in business indefinitely—"

"Moreover, the examples of the rich, scattered broadcast through the daily papers, hardly bear you out."

"They are the exception that proves the rule. Nine hundred and ninety-nine poor couples come to grief, and the world never hears of it. In the thousandth case a rich man and woman make fools of themselves and the world reads the scandal next morning. The principle is unaltered. The exceptions, the irresponsibles whether rich or poor, are something to which no rule applies."

"All right." Armstrong sat up, preventingly. "I don't want to argue with you. You're a typical lawyer and always ride me down by pure force of mass." He smiled. "Gentlemen of the law are invariably that way, Darley. Figuratively, you fellows always travel horseback while the rest of us go afoot, and if we don't hustle out of the way you ride us down without remorse."

Roberts was listening again in silence, with his normal attitude of passive observance.

"I'm feeling pretty spry, though, to-night," went on the other, "and able to get out of the way, so I'm going to get in close as possible and watch you. I've tried to do so before, but somehow I'm always side-tracked just at the psychological moment." The quizzical voice became serious, the flippant manner vanished. "Honestly, Darley, I can't understand you any more than you can me. You said a bit ago you wondered where I would end. I have the same wonder about you. Just what are you aiming at, old man, anyway? In all the years I've known you *you've* never come right out and said in so many words."

"You mean what do I intend to do that will make me famous or infamous, that will at least make me talked about?"

Armstrong laughed shortly. The shot was well aimed.

"I suppose that is approximately what I had in mind," he admitted.

"To answer your question then, directly, I don't intend to do anything. Nothing is further from my plans than to get a position where I'll be talked about."

"Just what do you want, then?"

"I want the substance, not the husk. I want to be the party that pulls the wires and not the figures that dance on the front of the stage. I want things done when I say they shall be done. I want the piper to play when I pass the word. I'm perfectly willing that others should have the honor and the glory and the limelight; but after the play is over I want to be the boy to whom the report is made and who gives directions for the next performance. Is that definite enough?"

"Yes, definite enough; but are you going to get there? You asked me the same question, you recall, a bit ago."

"Yes, if I live."

"And if you don't live?"

Again the shrug. "I shall have tried. I can tell Saint Peter that."

"I didn't refer to Saint Peter. I meant you yourself. Where is your own justification except in the attainment of the end?"

"Justification!" Roberts leaned suddenly forward, his attitude no longer that of an observer but of a participant, one in the front of the charge. "The game is its own justification, man! Things don't have to be done with two hundred bright young students watching and listening to be worth while, my friend."

Armstrong shifted uncomfortably, then he tacked.

14

"Just one more question, a repetition again of your own. Have you the attainment of this object you suggest definitely in sight? You're older than I and have been playing the game some time yourself."

"I think so."

"Do you know so?"

"As nearly as a man can know anything that hasn't come to pass."

"Just how, Darley? I'm absolutely in the dark in regard to your deals and I'm curious to know the inside. You've got something particular in mind, I know, or you wouldn't speak that way."

For the first time in minutes Roberts looked at the other, looked steadily, blankly.

"I'm sorry genuinely, Armstrong, but I can't tell you now. Don't misunderstand, please. I'd tell you if I were not under obligation; but I'm not at liberty yet to say." His glance left the other's face. "I trust you understand."

"Yes, certainly." The voice was short. "No offence, I'm sure."

That there was offence was obvious, yet Roberts made no further comment or explanation.

For perhaps a minute there was silence; in characteristic change of thought absolute Armstrong shifted.

"As long as we're in the confidant business," he digressed, "there's still one question I'd like to ask, Darley. Elice and I have been intimate now for a number of years. I've asked you repeatedly to call with me and you've always refused. Even yet you've barely met her. I quote you by the yard when I'm with her, and, frankly, she's — curious why you stay at arm's length. Between yourself and myself why is it, Darley?"

Roberts laughed; an instant later the light left his face.

"You know I have few women acquaintances," he said.

"I know, but this particular case is different."

"And those I do have," completed the other, "are all securely married."

Armstrong colored.

"I don't mean that," smiled Roberts, "and you know I don't. I'm not fool enough to fancy I'm a charmer. The explanation, I believe, is in my ancestry. I think they must have been fishes too, and instinct warns me to avoid bait. It's my own peace of mind I'm considering and preserving, friend Armstrong."

"Peace of mind!" the other laughed. "From you that's good, Darley. But the tape line—"

"Can't you find it?"

"I confess—You think there is a time then, after all, when it pays?"

"Do you fancy I show signs of feeble-mindedness?"

"No, emphatically not; but—Jove, you are human then after all! I begin to have hope."

Roberts stifled a yawn, a real yawn.

"I think I'll turn in," he said.

"Just a moment, Darley. I feel as though I'd discovered a gold mine, and I want to blaze its location before departing. Just when, with your philosophy, do you contemplate taking this important leap among the attached?"

Roberts looked at his companion in silence.

"Pardon me, Darley," swiftly, "that was flippant, I admit, but I'm really serious."

"Serious? I'll take you at your word. It'll be when I mean business, not pastime. Stretch the tape if you wish. There are some things it doesn't pay to play with. It'll be when I can give a woman the things, the material things, she wants and demands to make her happy and contented. The world is artificial, and material things are its reflection. When I can make the woman who chooses to marry me pass current anywhere, when I can be the means of giving her more pleasure, more opportunity, more of the good things of life than she has known before, then, when I know, not hope, this,—and not a minute before—Does that answer your question?"

"Yes; that's clear enough, I'm sure—the implication, too, for that matter." The speaker yawned, unnecessarily it seemed, for his look was keen. "By the way, though, you haven't given me a satisfactory explanation for avoiding Elice. She's attached practically, not unattached; and I personally want you to know her. I think it would make you understand some things you don't understand now. You might even approve of—dangling. What do you say, will you go out with me some evening or will you have another engagement as usual? I shan't suggest it again, Darley."

Standing, as he had risen a moment before, Darley Roberts looked down at the speaker steadily, the distinctive half-smile of tolerant analysis upon his lips. He laughed outright as though to clear the atmosphere.

"Certainly I'll go, Armstrong, if you wish. It never occurred to me before that you took it that way. I had supposed that you and Elice were an example of two being a company and three making a crowd; also, to change the simile, that previously your invitations were the proverbial crumbs of charity. I'll be pleased to go any time you wish."

"All right." Armstrong too had risen. "How about Sunday evening next week? Elice will be back Saturday."

"A week from Sunday; I shall not forget."

With the attitude of a big healthy animal, a bit sleepy now, Roberts stretched himself luxuriously, then started for his own room adjoining, calling back, "Good-night."

Armstrong watched him in silence until the other's hand was on the knob.

"Good-night," he echoed absently.

CHAPTER II

UNDERSTANDING

"What is it, Elice? You're transparent as spring water. Out with it."

"Out with what, Steve?"

"The secret information of vital importance that you're holding back with an effort for a favorable moment to deliver. The present isn't particularly dramatic, I'll admit, but it's the best circumstances permit."

"You're simply absurd, Steve; more so than usual."

"No, merely ordinarily observant. I've known you some time, and the symptoms are infallible. When you get that absent, beyond-earth look in your eyes, and sit twisting around and around that mammoth diamond ring your uncle gave you on your sixteenth birthday—Come, I'm impatient from the toes up. Who is engaged now?"

"No one, so far as I know."

"Married, then; don't try to fool me."

"Who told you, Steve Armstrong?"

"No one." The accompanying laugh was positively boyish. "I knew it was one or the other. Come, 'fess up. I'll be good, honest."

"You get younger every day, Steve," grudgingly. "If you keep on going backward people will be taking me for your mother soon instead of—merely myself."

"You shouldn't go away then, Elice. I'm tickled sick and irresponsible almost to have you back. I'm not to blame. But we're losing valuable time. I'm listening."

"You swear that you don't know already—that you aren't merely making fun of me?"

"On my honor as full professor of chemistry. I haven't even a suspicion."

"I wonder if you are serious—somehow I never know. I'll risk it anyway, and if you're just leading me on I'll never forgive you, Steve, never. It's Margery."

"Margery! The deuce it is—and Harry Randall, of course."

"Certainly. Who'd you think it was: Professor Wilson with his eight children?"

"Now I call that unkind, Elice. After all the interest I've shown, too! Honest, though, I am struck all in a heap. I never dreamed of such a thing—now."

The result of the revelation was adequate and Miss Gleason relented.

"It was rather 'sudden,' as they say. No one knew of it except their own families."

"Sudden! I should decidedly say so. I certainly thought they at least were to be depended upon, were standbys. When did it happen?"

"Last evening. Agnes Simpson just told me before you came."

"She did, did she? I thought she looked wondrous mysterious when I met her down the street. It was justifiable, though, under the circumstances. I suppose they, the Randalls, have gone away somewhere?"

"No; that's the funny part of it. They haven't gone and aren't going."

"Not at all?"

"No. I'm quoting Agnes."

"And why aren't they going? Did Agnes explain that?"

"Steve, you're horrid again."

"No; merely curious this time. Agnes is something of an authority, you'll admit."

"Yes; I guess I'll have to admit that. I didn't ask her, though, Steve Armstrong. She suggested gratis—that Harry couldn't afford it. They went into debt to buy furnishings for the house as it was."

"I don't doubt it. History pays even less than chemistry, and the Lord knows—No; I don't doubt it."

"Knows what, Steve?"

"Who knows what?"

"The one you suggested."

"Oh! I guess you caught the inference all right. No need to have put it in the abstract. We professors of the younger set are all in the same boat. We'd all have to go into debt under like circumstances."

Elice Gleason meditated.

"But Harry's been a full professor now a long time," she commented; "two years longer than you."

"And what difference does that make? He just lives on his salary."

"Is that so? I never thought of it that way. I don't think I ever considered the financial side before at all."

Armstrong looked his approval.

"I dare say not, Elice; and I for one am mighty glad you didn't. Life is cheap enough at best without adding to its cheapness unnecessarily."

The girl seemed scarcely to hear him, missing the argument entirely.

"I suppose, though," she commented reflectively, "when one does think of it, that it'll be rather hard on Margery to scrimp. She's always had everything she wants and isn't used to economizing."

Armstrong sat a moment in thought. He gave his habitual shrug.

"She should have thought of that before the minister came," he dismissed with finality. "It's a trifle late now."

"They've been putting it off for a long time, though," justified the girl, "and probably she thought—one has to cease delaying some time."

"Elice! Elice!" Armstrong laughed banteringly. "I believe you've got the June bug fluttering in your bonnet too. It's contagious this time of year, isn't it?"

"Shame on you, Steve!" The voice was dripping with reproach. "You always will be personal. You know I didn't mean it that way."

"Not a bit, honest now?"

"I say you ought to be ashamed to make fun of me that way."

"But honest—"

"Well," reluctantly, "maybe I did just a bit. We too have been engaged quite a while."

"Almost as long as the Randalls."

"Yes."

The quizzical look left Armstrong's eyes, but he said nothing.

"And I suppose every woman wants a home of her own. It's an instinct. I think I understand Margery."

From out the porch of the Gleason cottage, shaded from the curious by its climbing rose-vines, the girl looked forth at the sputtering electric globe on the corner.

"And, besides, people get to talking and smiling and making it unpleasant for a girl after so long. It was so with Margery. I know, although she never told me. It bothered her."

"You say after so long, Elice. How long?"

"I didn't mean any particular length of time, Steve. There isn't any rule by which you can measure gossip, so far as I know."

"Approximately, then."

"Oh, after a year, I suppose. It's about then that there's a comment or two sandwiched between the red and blue decks at bridge parties."

"And we've been engaged now three years. Do they ever sandwich—"

"How do I know. They don't do it to one's face."

"But Margery—you say they made it uncomfortable for her."

"Steve Armstrong," the voice was intentionally severe, "what possesses you to-night? I can't fancy what put that notion into your head."

"You did yourself," serenely, "just now. I never happened to stumble upon this particular continent before, and I'm intent on exploration and discovery. Honest, do they," he made an all-inclusive gesture, "talk about you and me?"

"I tell you they don't do those things to our faces."

"You're evading the question, girl Elice."

"They're not unpleasant intentionally."

"Still evasion. Out with it. Let's clear the air."

The girl drummed on the arm of her chair, first with one hand, then with the other. At last she looked the questioner fairly in the face.

"Frankly, Steve, they do; and they have for a year. But I don't mind. I didn't intend to say anything to you about it."

The look of the boy vanished from the other's eyes.

"I—see," he commented slowly.

"People are horrid that way, even people otherwise nice," amplified the girl. "As soon as any one they know has an—affair it immediately becomes public property. It's almost as bad as a murder case. The whole thing is tried and settled out of court."

The figure of the man settled down in his chair to the small of his back. His fingers locked over one knee.

"I suppose it was something of that kind Darley had in mind," he said.

"Darley Roberts? When?"

"We were talking about—similar cases a few days ago."

"You were?" There was just a shade of pique in the tone. "He must be a regular fount of wisdom. You're always quoting him."

"He is," tranquilly. "By the way, with your permission, he's going to call with me to-morrow night."

"With my permission!" The girl laughed. "You've solicited, and received, that several times before—and without result. I'm almost beginning to doubt the gentleman's existence."

"You won't much longer. I invited him and he accepted. He always does what he says he'll do."

"Very well," the voice was non-committal. "I'm always glad to meet any of your friends."

Armstrong warmed, as he always did when speaking of Darley Roberts.

"You will be when you know him, I'm sure. That's why I asked him to come. He's an odd chap and slow to thaw, but there isn't another lawyer in town, not even in the department, who's got his brains."

"They couldn't have, very well, could they?" evenly.

"I'll admit that was a trifle involved; but you know what I mean. He's what in an undergraduate they call a grind. The kind biographers describe as 'hewing forever to the line.' If we live and retain reasonably good health we'll hear of him some day."

"And I repeat," smilingly, "I've heard of him a great deal already."

Armstrong said nothing, which indicated mild irritation.

"Excuse me, Steve," said the girl, contritely. "I didn't mean to be sarcastic; that just slipped out. He has acted sort of queer, though, considering he's your room-mate and—I had that in mind. I am interested, however, really. Tell me about him."

Armstrong glanced at his companion; his gaze returned to his patent leather pumps, which he inspected with absent-minded concentration.

"I have told you before, I guess, about all I know. He's a good deal of an enigma to me, even yet."

"By the way, how did you happen to get acquainted with him, Steve?" From the manner spoken the question might or might not have been from genuine interest. "You've never told me that."

"Oh, it just happened, I guess. We were in the collegiate department together at first." He laughed shortly. "No, it didn't just happen either after all. I went more than half way—I recognize that now."

The girl said nothing.

"Looking back," continued the man, "I see the reason, too. He fascinated me then, as he does yet. I've had comparatively an easy enough sort of life. I was brought up in town, where there was nothing particular for a boy to do, and when it came college time my father backed me completely. Darley was the opposite exactly, and he interested me. He was unsocial; somehow that interested me more. I used to wonder why he was so when I first knew him; bit by bit I gathered his history and I wondered less. He's had a rough-and-tumble time of it from a youngster up." The voice halted suddenly, and the speaker looked at his companion equivocally. "Still interested, are you, Elice? I don't want to be a bore."

"Yes."

"I'll give you the story then as I've patched it together from time to time. I suppose he had parents once; but as they never figured, I infer they died when he was young. He came from the tall meadows out West straight to the University here. How he got the educational ambition I haven't the remotest idea; somehow he got it and somehow he came. It must have been a rub to make it. He's mentioned times of working on a farm, of chopping ties in Missouri, of heaving coal in a bituminous mine in Iowa, of—I don't know what all. And still he was only a boy when I first saw him; a great, big, over-aged boy with a big chin and bigger hands. The peculiar part is that he wasn't awkward and never has been. Even when he first showed up here green the boys never made a mark of him." Again the short expressive laugh. "I think perhaps they were a bit afraid of him."

"And he got right into the University?"

"Bless you, no; only tentatively. He had a lot of back work to make up at the academy. That didn't bother him apparently. He swallowed that and the regular course whole and cried for more." Armstrong stretched lazily. His hands sought his pockets. "I guess that's about all I know of the story," he completed.

"All except after he was graduated." It was interest genuine now.

"So you have begun to take notice at last," commented Armstrong, smilingly. "I'm a better *raconteur* than I imagined. When it comes to being specific, though, after he graduated, I admit I can't say much authoritatively. He'll talk about anything, ordinarily, except himself. I know of a dozen cases from the papers, some of them big ones, that he's been concerned in during the last few years; but he's never mentioned them to me. He seemed to get in right from the start. How he managed to turn the trick I haven't the slightest conception; he simply did. As I said before, he grows to be more of an enigma to me all the time."

Apparently the girl lost interest in the party under discussion; at least she asked no more questions and, dilatory as usual when not definitely directed, Armstrong dropped the lead. For a minute they sat so, gazing out into the night, silent. Under stimulus of a new thought, point blank, whimsical, came a change of subject.

"By the way," commented Armstrong, "I'm considering quitting the University and going into business, Elice. What do you think of the idea?"

"What—I beg your pardon, Steve."

The other repeated the question, all but soberly this time.

"Do you mean it, Steve, really, or are you just drawing me out?"

"Mean it!" Armstrong laughed. "Perhaps, and perhaps not. I don't know. What do you think of the notion, anyway?"

The girl looked at him steadily, a sudden wrinkle between her eyes.

"You have something special in mind, I judge, Steve; something I don't know about. What is it?"

"Special!" Armstrong laughed again, shortly this time. "Yes, I suppose so; though I didn't know it when I first asked the question. Now I'm uncertain—you take the suggestion so seriously. Graham, the specialty man, made me an offer to-day to go in with him. Five thousand dollars a year to start with, and a prospect of more later on."

The wrinkle between the girl's eyes smoothed. Her hands recrossed in her lap.

"You refused the offer, I judge," she said.

"No; that is, I told him I'd take the matter under advisement." Armstrong glanced at his companion swiftly; but she was not looking at him and he too stared out into the night. "I wanted to hear what you said about it first."

"Steve!"

In the darkness the man's face colored.

"Elice, aren't you—ashamed a bit to doubt me?"

"No." She was looking at him now smilingly. "I don't doubt you. I know you."

"You fancy I refused point blank, without waiting to tell you about it?"

For the third time the girl's fingers crossed and interlocked. That was all.

"Elice!" The man moved over to her, paused so, looking down into her face. "Tell me, I'm dead in earnest. Don't you trust me?"

"I trust you absolutely, Steve; but that doesn't prevent my knowing you."

"And I tell you I took the matter under advisement."

"He persuaded you to. You refused at first even to consider it."

Smilingly she returned his injured look fair in the eyes. Still smiling, she watched him as in silence he recrossed slowly to his place.

"Yes, you're right—as usual," he admitted at last. "You do know me. Apparently all my friends know me, better than I know myself." He shrugged characteristically. "But you haven't answered my question yet. What do you think of my accepting?"

"I try never to think—about the useless. You won't accept."

"You may be mistaken, may compel me to against my best judgment."

"No, you won't do that. I shan't influence you in the least."

For answer Armstrong stood up, his hands deep in his pockets, his shoulders square. A minute perhaps he stood so. Once he cleared his throat. He sat down. An instant later he laughed—naturally, in genuine amusement.

"I surrender, Elice," he said; "foot, horse, and officers. I can succeed in deceiving myself, easily; but when it comes to you—" He dropped his hands hopelessly. "On the square, though, and between ourselves, do you want me to quit the University and accept this—job? It's a good lead, I realize."

"I'd rather not say either way," slowly. "I repeat that it's useless to disagree, when nothing would be gained."

"Disagree! We never disagree. We never have in all the time we've known each other."

"We've never discussed things where disagreement was probable."

"Maybe that's right. I never thought of it before." A pause. "Has that harmony been premeditated on your part?"

"Unconsciously so, yes. It's an instinct with me, I think, to avoid the useless."

Armstrong stared across the dim light of the porch. Mentally he pinched himself.

"Well, I am dumb," he commented, "and you are wonderful. Let's break the rule, though, for once, and thresh this thing out. I want your opinion on this Graham matter, really. Tell me, please."

"Don't ask me," repeated the girl. "You'd remember what I said — and it wouldn't do any good. Let's forget it."

"Of course I'd remember. I want to remember," pressed the man. "You think I ought to accept?"

A moment the girl hesitated; then she looked him fair.

"Yes," she said simply.

"And why? Tell me exactly why, please? You're not afraid to tell me precisely what you think."

"No, I'm not afraid; but I think you ought to realize it without my putting it in words."

Armstrong looked genuine surprise.

"I suppose I ought—probably it's childishly obvious, but—tell me, Elice."

"To put it selfishly blunt, then, since you insist, I think you ought to for my sake. If an income you can depend upon means nothing in particular to you you might consider what it would mean to me."

Unconsciously the lounging figure of the man in the chair straightened itself. The drawl left his voice.

"Since we have stumbled upon this subject," he said quietly, "let's get to the bottom of it. I think probably it will be better for both of us. Just what would it mean to you, that five thousand dollars a year?"

"Don't you know, Steve, without my telling you?"

"Perhaps; but I'd rather you told me unmistakably."

As before the girl hesitated, longer this time; involuntarily she drew farther back until she was completely hidden in the shadow.

"What it means to me you can't help knowing, but I'll repeat it if you insist." She drew a long breath. Her voice lowered. "First of all, it would mean home, a home of my own. You don't know all that that means because you're a man, and no man really does understand; but to a woman it's the one thing supreme. You think I've got one now, have had all my life; but you don't know. Father and I live here. We keep up appearances the best we can; we both have pride. He holds his position in the University; out of charity every one knows, although no one is cruel enough to tell him so. We manage to get along somehow and keep the roof tight; but it isn't living, it isn't home. It's a perpetual struggle to make ends meet. His time of usefulness is past, as yours will be past when you're his age; and it's been past for years. I never admitted this to a human being before, but I'm telling it to you because it's true. We've kept up this—fight for years, ever since I can remember, it seems to me. We've never had income enough to go around. I haven't had a new dress in a year. I haven't the heart to ask for it. Everything I have has been darned and patched and turned until it won't turn again. It isn't poverty such as they have on the East Side, because it isn't frank and open and aboveboard; but it's genteel poverty in the best street of the town: University Row. It's worse, Steve, because it's unadmitted, eternally concealed, hopeless. It isn't a physical hunger, but again a worse one: an artistic hunger. I'm a college graduate with letters on the end of my name when I choose to use them. I've mixed with people, seen the niceties of life that only means can give, couldn't help seeing them; and they're all beyond my reach, even the common ones. If I didn't know anything different I shouldn't feel the lack; but I do know. I'm not even to blame for knowing. It was inevitable, thrust upon me. I'm the hungry child outside the baker's window. I can look and look—and that is all."

The voice ceased. Frankly, unhesitatingly, the face came out of the shadow and remained there.

"I think you understand now what I mean, Steve, unmistakably. I suppose, too, you think me selfish and artificial and horrid, and I shan't deny it. I am as I am and I want things. To pretend that I don't would be to lie—and I won't lie to you whatever happens. I simply won't. We both know what your place in the University means; I perhaps better than you, because I've seen my father's experience. I don't often get bitter, but I come very near it when I look back and think how my mother had to plan and scrimp. I feel like condemning the whole University to the bottomless pit. I suppose Margery Randall would resent it if I told her so, but honestly I pity her; the more so because I've always envied her in a way. She's not used to denying herself anything, and there's bound to be a reckoning. It's inevitable, and then—I don't like to think of how it will be then. It's a tragedy, Steve, nothing more or less."

Opposite the man sat motionless in his place looking at her. All trace of his usual lounging attitude was absent. He was not even smoking. For almost a full minute after she was done he sat; then he arose abruptly. This time he did not offer to come over to her.

"So this is the way you feel," he commented at last, slowly. "It's a new phase of you entirely, Elice, that I admit; but at least I'm glad to know it." He thrust his hands deep into his pockets. "In plain English, you'd barter my position and ambition gladly for—things. Frankly I didn't think that of you, Elice, before. I imagined I knew you better, knew different."

Responsive, instinctively the girl started to rise. Her breath came quick. Swiftly following came second thought and she sank back, back into the shadow. She said nothing.

A moment the man waited, expecting an answer, a denial, something; when nothing came he put on his hat with meaning deliberation.

"I repeat I'm very glad you told me, though, even if I do have to readjust things a bit." He shrugged his shoulders. Despite the wounded egotism that was urging him on, it was the first real cloud that had arisen on the horizon of their engagement and he was acutely self-conscious. "Rest assured, however, that I shall consider your point of view before I say yes or no to Graham. Just now —" He halted, cleared his throat needlessly; abruptly, without completing the sentence or giving a backward glance, he started down the walk. "Good-night, Elice," he said.

CHAPTER III

PLEASURE

"The trouble with you, Darley," said Armstrong, "is that you took your course in the University in too big doses. You went on the principle that if a little grinding is good for a man a perpetual dig must be a great deal better." He was in the best of humor this Sunday night, and smiled at the other genially. "A college course is a good deal like strychnine. Taken in small doses over a long period of time it is a great tonic. Swallowed all at once—you know what happens."

From her place in a big easy chair Elice Gleason watched with interest the result of the badinage, but Roberts himself made no comment.

"You started in," continued Armstrong, "to do six years' work in four—and did it. You were a human grinding machine and you ground very fine, that I'll admit; but in doing so you missed a lot that was more valuable, a lot that while it doesn't make credit figures in the sum total of university atmosphere."

"For instance?" suggested the other, laconically.

"Well, for one thing, you never joined a fraternity. I know," quickly, "that the frats are abused, as every good thing is abused, but fundamentally they're good. When it comes to humanizing a man, rounding him out, which is the purpose of college life, they're just as essential as a course in the sciences."

"Unfortunately," commented Roberts, drily, "the attitude of a student to the Greeks is a good deal like that of woman to man. She can't marry until she is asked. I was likewise never sufficiently urged."

"In that case," laughed Armstrong, "I'll have to acquit you on that count. There wasn't, however, anything to prevent you warming up socially. No student has to be asked to do that. You and Elice, for instance, took your courses at the same time. Normally you would have met at social doings on a hundred occasions; and still you have never really done so until to-night, several years after you were graduated. You can't square yourself on that score."

"No," acquiesced Roberts with judicial slowness; "and still a man with one suit of clothes and that decidedly frayed at the seams labors under appreciable social disadvantages even in a democratic university." He smiled, a tolerant, reminiscent smile. "I recall participating tentatively a bit early in my career, but the result was not entirely a success. My stock went below par with surprising rapidity; so I took it off the market."

Armstrong glanced at the listening girl swiftly. Purposely he was trying to draw the other man out—and for her benefit. But whatever the girl was thinking her face was non-committal. He returned to the attack.

"All right," he shifted easily; "we'll pass charge number two likewise. One thing at least, however, you'll admit you could have done. You might have taken up athletics. You were asked often enough, I know personally—nature did a lot for you in some things; and as for clothes—the fewer you have in athletics the better. You could have mixed there and warmed up to your heart's content. Isn't it so?"

This time Roberts laughed.

"I was engaged in athletics—all the time I was in the University," he refuted.

"The deuce you were! I never knew before—All right, I bit. How was that, Darley?"

"Simple enough, I'm sure," drily. "I venture the proposition that I sawed more wood and stoked more furnaces during my course than any other student that ever matriculated. I had four on the string constantly."

Armstrong sank back in his chair lazily.

"All right, Darley," he accepted; "when you won't be serious there's no use trying to make you so. I surrender."

"Serious!" Roberts looked at the younger man peculiarly. "Serious!" he echoed low. "That's just where your diagnosis fails, my friend. It's the explanation as well why I never did those 'other things,' as you call them, that students do and so humanize themselves." Involuntarily his eyes went to the girl's face, searched it with a glance. "It is, I suppose, the curse of my life: the fact that I can't be different. I seem to be incapable of digressing, even if I want to."

For answer Armstrong smiled his sceptical smile; but the girl did not notice. Instead, for the first time, she asked a question.

"And you still think to digress, to enjoy oneself, is not serious, Mr. Roberts?" she asked.

"No, emphatically not. I'm human, I hope, even if I haven't been humanized. I think enjoyment of life by the individual is its chief end. It's nature."

"But you said—"

"Pardon me," quickly; "I couldn't have made myself clear then. We're each of us a law unto himself, Miss Gleason. What is pleasure to me, perhaps, is not pleasure to you. I said I was never asked to join a fraternity. It's true. It's equally true, though, that I wouldn't have joined had I been asked. So with the social side. I wouldn't have been a society man if I'd had a new dress suit annually and a valet to keep it pressed. I simply was not originally bent that way. Killing time, politely called recreation, merely fails to afford me pleasure. For that reason I avoid it. I claim no credit for so doing. It's not consecration to duty at all, it's pure selfishness. I'm as material as a steam engine. My pleasure comes from doing things; material things, practical things. For a given period of time my pleasure is in being able to point to a given object accomplished and say to myself: there, 'Darley, old man, you started out to do it and you've done it.' Is that clear, Miss Gleason?"

"And if you don't accomplish it, what then?" commented Armstrong.

"I shall at least have tried," returned the other, carelessly. "I can call the attention of Saint Peter to that fact."

Armstrong leaned back farther in his chair. His eyes sought the ceiling whimsically.

"That would naturally bring up the old problem," he philosophized, "of whether it were better to attempt to do a thing and fail or not to make the attempt and retain one's self-confidence."

In her place the girl shifted restlessly, as though the digression annoyed her.

"To return to the starting point," she said, "you think the greatest pleasure in life is in action, not in passive sensation? We lazy folks—"

"Pardon me," interrupted Armstrong, "but I want to anticipate and enter an objection. Some of us aren't lazy. We're merely economical of our energies."

"We lazy folks," repeated the girl, evenly, "are sometimes inclined to think differently."

This time Roberts hesitated, his face a blank as he studied the two before him. Just perceptibly he leaned forward. His big hands closed on the chair arms.

"Are you really interested in hearing the definition of pleasure as I have formulated it for myself, Miss Gleason?" he asked; "I repeat, as I have formulated it for myself?"

"Yes."

Again Roberts hesitated, his face inscrutable, his body motionless as one asleep.

"Pleasure," he began low, "is power; conscious, unquestionable, superior power. In a small way we all experience it when we are hungry and have the ability to satisfy that hunger. The big animal feels it when the lesser animal is within its reach and the big animal knows it. The lover tastes it when he knows another returns that love completely, irresistibly—knows, I say. The student comprehends it when he is conscious of ability to solve the problem presented, to solve it unqualifiedly. The master of men realizes it when those in his command obey him implicitly; when his word is law. Pleasure is not necessarily an exercise of that power, in fact is not generally so; but it lies in the consciousness of ability to exercise it at will. For the big animal to annihilate the less would bring pain, not pleasure. Hunger satisfied is passivity, not pleasure. And so on down the list. Superior, conscious power exercised defeats its own purpose. It is, as men say, unsportsmanlike. Held in reserve, passive, completely under control, it makes of a human being a god. This to me is pleasure, Miss Gleason."

For a moment after he ceased speaking the room was quiet. Armstrong still sat staring at the ceiling; but the smile had left his lips. The girl was watching the visitor frankly, the tiny pucker, that meant concentration, between her eyebrows. Roberts himself broke the silence.

"You've heard my definition, Miss Gleason," he laughed; "and no doubt think me a savage or something of that kind. I shan't attempt to deny it if you do either. Just as a matter of curiosity and of interest, though, so long as the subject is up, I'd like to hear your own definition." Of a sudden he remembered. "And yours, too, Armstrong," he added.

The wrinkle vanished from the girl's forehead. She smiled in turn. An observer might have said she sparred for time. "After you, Steve," she accepted.

Armstrong shifted in his seat elaborately.

"This is indeed a bit sudden," he remarked in whimsical commonplace, "however—" His hands went into his pockets automatically. His eyes followed a seam on the paper overhead back and forth, before halting preparatorily.

"Pleasure with me," he began, "is not practical, but very much the reverse." His lips twitched humorously. "Neither has it reference to any superior power. I wouldn't give one single round penny, providing I had it, to be able to whistle and have a thousand of my fellows dance to the tune—against their wishes. If I could whistle so sweetly or so enchantingly that they'd caper nimbly because they wanted to, because the contagion was irresistible, then—" The whimsical look passed as suddenly as it had come. "Pleasure with me, I think," he continued soberly, "means appreciation by my fellow-men, in big things and in little things. I'm a kind of sunflower, and that is my sun. I'd like to be able to play marbles so well that the kids would stare in amazement; to fashion such entrancing mud pies that the little girls would want to eat them; to play ball so cleverly that the boys would always choose me first in making up sides; to dance so divinely that the girls would dream about it afterward; to tell so entertaining a story that men would let their cigars go dead while they listened, or under different circumstances the ladies would split their gloves applauding—if they happened to have them on; last of all, to write a novel so different and interesting that the reading public, and that means every one, would look on the cover after they'd turned the last sheet to see who the deuce did it; then trim the lamp afresh, loosen their collar comfortably and read it through again. This to me spells pleasure in capitals all the way through: plain appreciation, pure and simple, neither more nor less."

Again silence followed, but a far different silence than before. Of that difference the three in the room were each acutely conscious; yet no one made comment. They merely waited, waited until, without preface, the girl completed the tacit agreement.

"And pleasure to me," she said slowly, "means something different than it does to either of you. In a way, with you both pleasure is active. With me it's passive." She laughed shortly, almost nervously. "Maybe I'm lazy, I don't know; but I've worked so long that I'm weary to death of commonplace and repression and denial and—dinginess. I want to be a free individual and have leisure and opportunity to feel things, not to do them. I'm selfish, hopelessly selfish, morbidly selfish; but I am as I am. I'm like the plant that's raised in a cellar and can't leave because its roots are sunk there deep. I want to be transplanted perforce out into the sunshine. I'm hungry for it, hungry. I've caught glimpses of things beyond through my cellar window, but glimpses only. I repeat, I want to feel unhampered. I know pretty things and artistic things when I see them, and I want them: to wear, to live among, to look at. I want to travel, to hear real music, to feel real operas and know real plays— not imitations. I'm tired of reading about life and hearing about life. I want to live it, be a part of it—not a distant spectator. That is what pleasure means to me now; to escape the tyranny of repression and of pennies and be free—free!"

"I'm tired of reading about life and hearing about life. I want to live it"

For the third time silence fell; a silence that lasted longer far than before, a silence which each was loth to break. While she was speaking, at first Armstrong had shifted about in his chair restlessly; at the last, his hands deep in his pockets, he had sat still. Once he had looked at her, peculiarly, the tolerant half smile still on his lips; but she had not returned the look, and bit by bit it vanished. That was all.

For a minute perhaps, until it became awkward at least, the silence lasted—to be broken finally by the girl herself. Slowly she arose from her seat and, tall, slender, deliberately graceful, came from her place in the shadow into the light.

"I'm a bit ashamed to have brought out the family skeleton and aired it to-night," she said evenly. Under drooping lids she looked from one face before her to the other swiftly. "I don't know why I did it exactly. I'm a bit irresponsible, I guess, to-night. We are all so, I think, at times." As deliberately as she did everything she took a seat. Her hands folded in her lap. "If you'll forget it I'll promise not to offend in the same way again." She smiled and changed the subject abruptly. "I see by the papers," she digressed, "that at last we're to have a trolley line in town. The same authority informs us as well that you are the moving spirit, Mr. Roberts."

"Yes." It was the ordinary laconic, non-committal man of business who answered. A pause, then a significant amplification. "This is the age of the trolley. There are a hundred miles of suburban lines contracted for as well. No one will recognize this country as it is now ten years hence."

"And this suburban line you speak of—I suppose you're the spirit back of that too?" queried the girl.

"Yes." This time there was no amplification.

"So that was what you had in mind the other night when we were talking,—what you wouldn't tell me," commented Armstrong, a shade frostily.

"One thing, yes." Roberts ignored the tone absolutely. "I was not at liberty to make the announcement at that time. The deal was just closed last night."

Armstrong made no further comment, but his high spirits of the early evening had vanished not to return, and shortly thereafter Roberts arose to go. Promptly, seemingly intentionally so, Armstrong followed. In the vestibule, his hat in his hand, by design or chance he caught the visitor's eye.

"Pardon me a moment," he apologized, "I—forgot something."

Perforce Roberts waited while the other man returned to the tiny library they had just vacated. The girl was standing within precisely as when they had left and, as Armstrong did not close the door, the visitor knew to a certainty that his presence as listener and spectator was intentional. It was all a premeditated scene, the climax of the evening.

"By the way, Elice," said the actor, evenly, "I've been considering that Graham offer carefully since I spoke to you about it the other night." He did not look at her but stood twirling his hat judicially in his hand. "I tried to convince myself that it was for the best to accept; but I failed. I told him so to-day."

There was a pause.

"Yes," suggested the girl.

Another pause.

"I hope you're not—disappointed, Elice."

Still another pause, appreciable, though shorter than before.

"No; I'm not disappointed," replied the girl then. At last Armstrong had glanced up and, without looking himself, the listener knew as well as though he had seen that the speaker was smiling steadily. "I'm not disappointed in the least, Steve."

CHAPTER IV

UNCERTAINTY

It was ten minutes after three on the following afternoon when Stephen Armstrong, in the lightest of flannels and jauntiest of butterfly ties, strolled up the tree-lined avenue and with an air of comfortable proprietorship wandered in at the Gleason cottage. A movable sprinkler was playing busily on the front lawn and, observing that the surrounding sod was well soaked, with lazy deliberation he shifted it to a new quarter. As he approached the house a mother wren flitted away before his face, and at the new suggestion he stood peering up at the angle under the eaves for the nest that he knew was near about. Once, standing there with the hot afternoon sun beating down upon him, he whistled in imitation of the tiny bird's call; nothing developing, he mounted the steps and pulled the old-fashioned knocker familiarly.

There was no immediate response and he pulled again; without waiting for an answer, he dropped into the ever-convenient hammock stretched beside the door and swung back and forth luxuriously. Unconsciously, and for the same reason that a bird sings—because it is carelessly oblivious of anything save the happiness of the moment—he began whistling softly to himself: without definite time or metre, subconsciously improvising. Perhaps a dozen times he swung back and forth; then the whistling ceased.

"Anything doing at this restaurant this afternoon, Elice?" he plunged without preface. An expansive smile made up for the lack of conventional greeting. "I'm as hungry as those little wrens I hear cheeping up there somewhere."

The smile was contagious and the girl returned it unconsciously.

"I believe you're always hungry, Steve Armstrong," she commented.

"I know it. I was born that way."

"And you never grew up."

"Physically, yes, unfortunately. Otherwise—I'm fighting to the last ditch. I believe about three of those cookies you make—and, by the way, they're much better than mother used to manufacture—will fill the void. Don't you hear that cheeping?"

The girl hesitated, disappeared, and returned.

"Thank you, Elice. Sit down over there, please, where I can see you. It makes them taste better. That's right. Thank you, again. I'm going to pay my bill now by telling you your fortune. You're going to make a great cook."

"I wonder," said the girl, enigmatically.

"There's no question about it. And for good measure I'm going to retail the latest gossip. What, by the way and as a preliminary, do you suppose I've been doing all day?"

"It's vacation. Fishing, I presume."

"Stung! I did go fishing this morning—four o'clock, caught one too; but it was so small and innocent looking that I apologized and threw it back. That wasn't what I referred to, however. You'll have to guess again."

"I haven't the slightest idea."

"I'm compelled to assist you then. I've been helping the Randalls settle. Harry 'phoned me early this morning and wanted to know if I didn't desire to be useful; said he would exchange compliments sometime." A significant pause, then a reminiscent sigh. "Every vertebra in my spinal column aches with an individual and peculiar pain."

"They're really settled at last, are they?" inquired the girl, interestedly. "I can hardly wait to see how things look."

"I don't blame you for being curious, Elice," sympathized Armstrong. "I felt a bit the same way myself." A rueful grin. "Merely among ourselves, however, and as a word of advice between friends, you'd better curb your impatience for about a week longer."

"And why? You're darkly mysterious, as usual."

"Mysterious! Heavens, no; merely compassionate." He held up his hand for inspection. "Look at that blister. It's as big as a dime and feels like a prune. They're not done yet and they'd induce you to duplicate it if they ever got you into their clutches. So long as it's all in the family I think one blister is about sufficient. Better lay low for a week anyway."

"Steve," the voice was severe, "you're simply impossible. They'd never forgive you if they knew you talked that way."

"Yes, they would," easily. "I promised to come back and help complete the job." Of a sudden he laughed boyishly, reminiscently. "Seriously, Elice, I've had a memorable day." He laughed again. "Pardon me, but I've wanted to do that for hours and didn't dare. Such a mixture of furnishings as those two people have accumulated you never saw brought together under one roof before in your life."

"Mixture, how? I fail to see the joke."

"You will when you visit them, all right. I warn you in advance to be discreet." He looked at his companion with whimsical directness. "You see it was this way. They started out together to buy things, with Margery at the helm. She's not accustomed particularly to consider cost and went at the job with avidity. She's methodical also, you know, and began at the front door. In fancy she entered the reception hall, and the first need that appealed to her was a rug. She picked out one. It's Oriental, and a beauty: cost one hundred dollars if a cent. Next, in her mind's eye, she noticed the bare windows— curtains were required, of course. So she selected them. They're the real thing and two pairs—another hundred, I'll wager. Following came three or four big leather chairs—nothing better in town. I can fancy old Harry's heart sinking by this time; but he didn't say a word—yet. Margery took another spurt and went on to the living-room. In consequence another big rug—and another hundred withdrawn from circulation. A jolly big davenport—more curtains;—and then something happened. They told me so, but I didn't need to be told; for it was then that Harry butted in. They were bankrupt already, and he knew it. He simply had to call a halt.

It's the funniest contrast I ever saw, and pathetic too; for from this point on the whole house is a nightmare. Cheap! he bought the cheapest things he could find and even then he got scared. By the time they got through the dining-room he must have been a nervous wreck, for the kitchen and upstairs furniture is second-hand, every stick and frying pan; and even then—" The humor left the speaker's face. "It's a shame to make fun of it, though, Elice. They're going to replace it all as soon as they can."

For a moment neither said anything.

"And Margery?" suggested the girl at last.

"That's where the little tragedy crops out. You see we began the way she had begun—at the front door. She was pleased as a boy with new boots at the reception hall. Still cheerful over the living-room. Non-committal in the diner. From there on Harry and I carted things upstairs and juggled with them alone and according to our own ideas."

For the second time there was silence; then, low-voiced, came another suggestion.

"And—Harry?"

"He's game," admiringly. "He may be thinking a lot—I've no doubt he is; but he's not letting out a peep or making a sign. He pretended Margery was just tired out and bundled her out of doors under the trees. That's one thing they've got at least: a whole yard full of grandfather elms. He sort of looked at me cross-eyed while he was doing it to see if I caught on, but I was blind as a post. By the way, I nearly forgot to mention it, but you and I are invited there for dinner this coming Thursday—sort of a house-warming and appreciation of my efforts combined."

"For dinner, so soon?" The girl stared incredulously. "I don't believe Margery ever cooked a meal in her life."

"She isn't going to try to yet, she informed me, so be of good cheer. That sort of thing is all to come later on, with the replaced furniture. At present she's to have a maid and take observations." The speaker laughed characteristically. "I asked her if she referred to the sort of individual my mother used to call a hired girl, but she stuck to 'maid.' It seems they are to pay her six dollars a week. Hired girls only command four."

Elice Gleason joined in the laugh sympathetically. The other's good spirits was irresistible.

"You seem to have been gathering valuable data," she commented drily.

"I have indeed. I couldn't well help it. I was even forced into the conviction that it was intended I should so gather." He smiled into his companion's eyes whimsically. "They're deep, those Randalls. After all is said I fancy my assistance was acquired not so much from any desire to save as to point a valuable object lesson; scatter the contagion, as it were." He paused meaningly and smiled again. "Elice mine, we're in grave danger, you and I. That worthy pair have designs upon our future. They are in the position of a certain class, famed in adage, who desire company. The dinner is only another illustration of the same point."

Elice Gleason returned the smile, but quietly. She made no further comment, however, and the subject dropped.

In the hammock Armstrong swung back and forth in lazy well-being. Overhead the mother wren, a mere brown shadow, flitted in return over their heads. There was an instant's clamor from hidden fledglings, and silence as the shadow passed back once more into the sunshine. Watching through half-closed eyes, comfortably whimsical, Armstrong gazed into space where the shadow had vanished.

"What a responsibility the care of a family must be," he commented, "particularly in this hot weather. That wren certainly has my sympathy—and respect." He paused to give the swinging hammock a fresh impulse. "I wonder though," he drifted on, "that is, if it is permissible to tangle up a variety of thoughts, if it's any harder than it is to attempt to pull an idea out of one's self by the roots and work it up into readable form with the thermometer above ninety in the shade—I wonder."

Elice Gleason was observing him now, peculiarly, understandingly.

"How is the book coming, anyway, Steve?" she asked directly.

"Which book?" smilingly.

"*The* book, of course."

"They're all *the* books—or were at one time." A trace, the first, of irony crept into his voice. "To be specific, however, masterpiece number one has just completed its eighteenth round trip East, and is taking a deserved rest. Masterpiece number two is *en route* somewhere between here and New York, either coming or going, on its eleventh journey. Number three has only five tallies to its credit— but hope springs eternal. Number four, the baby, still adolescent, has temporarily halted in its growth while I succor a needy benedict friend in distress. I believe that covers the family."

The characterization was typically nonsensical; but, sympathetic, the listener read between the sentences and understood.

"Isn't the new one coming well?" she asked low. "Tell me, Steve, honest."

"Coming well, Elice! What a question to ask of probably America's foremost living writer!" The speaker was still smiling. "What reprehensible misgiving, suspicion even!" Sudden silence, wherein bit by bit the smile faded. Silence continued until in its place came a new expression, one that changed the boy's face absolutely, made it a man's face—and not a young one at that.

"Coming well, Elice?" he repeated. "Honest, as you say, I don't know." The hammock had become still, but the speaker did not notice, merely lying there looking up into the sunshine and the blue unseeingly. "Sometimes I think it is, and then again—if one could only know about such things, know, not hope—of course every writer in his own soul fancies—and his friends, for that matter, are just about as useful—" The speaker drew himself together with a shrug. For an instant his jaw locked decisively.

"I know I'm more or less irresponsible, as a rule, Elice," he analyzed swiftly, "and probably create the impression that I'm even more irresponsible than I am; but in this thing, at least, I'm serious. From the bottom of my soul I want to write well, want to. As I said before, sometimes I think I can—auto-intoxication maybe it is, I don't know—and I'm as happy as a child, or a god, or a bird, or any completely happy thing you can fancy. Then again, as it's been the past week, or the past month for that matter, I don't seem to be able to do anything new. On top of this everything I've already done fairly personifies and leers at me. I get so that I fairly hate myself for the utter failure that I am, that at least I have been so far. I get to analyzing myself; I can't help it, and the result isn't pleasant. I've been doing so lately. I don't overestimate myself in the least, Elice girl. Practically, commercially, I'm a zero. I'm simply not built that way. If I'm ever of any use in the world, ever amount to anything whatever, it will be in an impractical, artistic way. Whether I'll ever win out so—oh, for light, for light!... Frankly, the new novel is going badly, Elice, cursedly bad!"

"I'm sorry, Steve. You know—"

"Yes, I know."

"I've believed always, and still believe—"

"Yes, I know that too."

"You've got it in you to win; I know it, and you know it. You've done good work already, lots of it, and—"

"Wade into him and lick him!" bitterly. "He's only three sizes larger than you are, and afraid—I know you can lick him. Wade in!"

The girl said nothing.

"Forgive me, Elice," with quick contrition. "That was nasty of me, I confess. But I'm sore to-day, raw. It's genius I suppose," sarcastically, "genius unappreciated."

Still the girl said nothing.

"If I could only get a ray of light, a lead, the flutter of a signal from outside the wall. But I keep hammering my head at it day after day, and it remains precisely as it was years ago when I began. It's maddening."

Yet the girl was silent, waiting silent.

"And, last of all, if I should eventually succeed, should break through into my own, as Darley Roberts says, even then—from any point of view it isn't a cheerful prospect."

"As Mr. Roberts says? What was that, Steve?"

"I referred to the reward, pecuniary reward. He figured it out in dollars and cents once when he wanted to bring me out of the clouds. Looking at it that way, there isn't much to the game even for the winners, Elice."

"Not much if you win? I can't believe it, Steve. I always supposed—"

"Everybody does. The public, the uninitiated, are long on supposing. Even the would-be's like myself delude themselves and build air castles until some hard-headed friend calls the turn. Then—no; there really isn't much in it, Elice; nothing in comparison to the plums in the business world. That job of Graham's, for instance, offers greater possibilities than success even, and when it comes to partial success or failure! It's a joke, the artistic temperament in this commercial twentieth century, a tremendous side-splitting joke! One nowadays should be born with suckers on his fingers, such as a fly has on its feet, so that whenever he came into the vicinity of a bank note it would stick fast. That would be the ideal condition, the greatest natural blessing, now!"

"You know you don't mean that, Steve. It's hot and you're out of the mood to-day—that's all. To-morrow will be different; you'll see things straight again."

"Thank you, Elice. You're right, as usual. I said I was raw to-day. It's boyish to be so too, I realize that. But it's hard sometimes, deucedly hard, when others are doing something and getting somewhere to see yourself standing still. One gets to thinking and imagining things that probably don't exist." He took a long breath. "It's this thing of imagination that's worse than reality. It crawls in between everything so; and somehow you can't keep it out. It gives one a scare." He laughed shortly, ill at ease. "It even makes one doubt a little the people one believes in most: take you and me, for instance. In my sane moments I know nothing could get between us; but sometimes I get to imagining—times like the last few days when I am—raw—that we're gradually drifting apart. A little difference of opinion comes up and imagination magnifies until it becomes a mountain and—I know I'm preposterous, Elice, and there's nothing really to it, but the thing's been on my mind and I wanted to tell you and get it out of my system." He had hurried on, leading up to the point, making the situation deliberately. Now he turned to her, smiling frankly. "It's preposterous, isn't it, Elice? Tell me so. I like to hear you say it."

"Preposterous, Steve?" The girl returned the look, but for some reason, probably one she herself could not have told, she did not smile. She merely looked at him, steadily, unwaveringly. "I have never thought of the possibility before, never questioned. Certainly nothing has come between us. To imagine—I never imagine the unpleasant, Steve."

The figure in the hammock shifted restlessly, as though but half satisfied.

"And nothing ever will, Elice?" he pressed. "Say that just to please me. I think an awful lot of you, girl; so much that at times I'm afraid."

This time the girl smiled, quietly, very quietly.

"And I of you, Steve," she echoed. "Must I protest that?"

"No," swiftly, "not for an instant. I don't doubt, mind…. It's all that cursed imagination of mine. I was only thinking of the future. If things shouldn't come my way, shouldn't—I put it at the worst possible—if by any chance I should remain a—failure such as I am now—you wouldn't mind—would overlook—it wouldn't make any difference at all with you and me, would it, Elice?"

"Steve, you mustn't say such things—mustn't, I say. It's morbid. I won't listen."

"But tell me," passionately, "what I asked. I want to hear you say it. I want to know."

For an instant the girl was silent, an instant that seemed minutes to the expectant listener. For the second time she met him eye to eye.

"Whether or not you become famous as a writer," she said slowly, "won't make any difference in the least. It's you I care for, Steve; you as you are now and nothing more." The voice paused but the eyes did not shift. "As for the future, Steve man, I can't promise nor can you. To do so would be to lie, and I won't lie. I say I love you; you as you are. If anything ever should come between us, should, I say— you suggested it and—persist—it will be because of a change in you yourself." For the second time she halted; then she smiled. "I think that's all there is to say," she completed.

"All!" With a buoyancy unfeigned the man swung out of the hammock upon his feet. "That's just the beginning. You're just getting under way, Elice."

"No," peremptorily; "all—for the present at least. It's four o'clock of the afternoon, you know, and the neighbors have eyes like—Look at the sun shine!... You've scared away the wren too, and the brood is hungry. Besides it's time to begin dinner. Cooks shouldn't be hindered ever." She turned toward the door decisively. "You may stay if you don't bother again," she smiled over her shoulder. "Meanwhile there's a new 'Life' and a July 'Century,'—you know where," and with a final smile she was gone.

CHAPTER V

CERTAINTY

Four months had drifted by; again the University was in full swing.

Of an evening in late October at this time, in the common living-room which joined the two private rooms in the suite occupied by himself and Darley Roberts, Stephen Armstrong was alone. It was now nearly eleven o'clock, and he had come in directly after dinner, ample time to have prepared his work for the next day; but as yet he had made no move in that direction. On the roll-top desk, with its convenient drop light, was an armful of reference books and two late scientific magazines. They were still untouched, however, bound tight by the strap with which they had been carried.

But one sign of his prolonged presence was visible in the room. That, a loose pile of manuscript alternately hastily scribbled and painfully exact, told of the varying moods under which it had been produced;—that and a tiny pile of cigarette stumps in the nearby ash-tray, some scarcely lit and others burned to a tiny stump, which had become the manuscripts' invariable companion.

For more than an hour now, however, he had not been writing. The night was frosty and he had lit the gas in the imitation fireplace. The open flame had proved compellingly fascinating and, once stretched comfortably in the big Turkish rocker before it, duty had called less and less insistently and there he had remained. For half an hour thereafter he had scarcely stirred; then, without warning, he had risen. On the mantel above the grate was a collection of articles indigenous to a bachelor's den: a box half filled with cigars, a jar of tobacco, a collection of pipes, a cut-glass decanter shaded dull red in the electric light. It was toward the latter that he turned, not by chance but with definite purpose, and without hesitation poured a whiskey glass level full. There was no attendant siphon or water convenient and he drank the liquor raw and returned the glass to its place. It was not the quasi-æsthetic tippling of comradery but the deliberate drinking of one with a cause, real or fancied, therefor and

51

for its effect; and as he drank he shivered involuntarily with the instinctive aversion to raw liquor of one to whom the action has not become habitual. Afterward he remained standing for a moment while his eyes wandered aimlessly around the familiar room. As he did so his glance fell upon the pile of text-books, mute reminder of a lecture yet unprepared, and for an instant he stood undecided. With a characteristic shrug of distaste and annoyance, of dismissal as well, he resumed his seat, his slippered feet spread wide to catch the heat.

Another half-hour passed so, the room silent save for the deliberate ticking of a big wall clock and the purr of the gas in the grate; at last came an interruption: the metallic clicking of a latch key, the tramp of a man's feet in the vestibule, and Darley Roberts entered. A moment after entering the newcomer paused attentive, his glance taking in every detail of the all too familiar scene; deliberately, as usual, he hung up his top-coat and hat.

"Taking it comfortable-like, I see," he commented easily as he pulled up a second chair before the grate. "Knocked off for the evening, have you?"

"Knocked off?" Armstrong shrugged. "I hardly know. I haven't knocked on yet. I'm stuck in the mud, so to speak."

Roberts drew the customary black cigar from his waistcoat pocket and clipped the end methodically. As he did so, apparently by chance, his glance swept the mantel above the grate, and, returning, took in the testimony of the desk with its unopened text-books and pile of scattered manuscript. Equally without haste he lit a match and puffed until the weed was well aglow.

"Any assistance a friend can give?" he proffered directly. "We all get tangled at times, I guess. At least every one I know does."

Armstrong's gaze left the fire and fastened on his companion peculiarly.

"Do you yourself?" he asked bluntly.

"Often."

"That's news. I fancied you were immune. What, if I may ask, do you do at such times to effect your release?"

"Go to bed, ordinarily, and sleep while the mud is drying up. There's usually a big improvement by morning."

"And when there isn't—"

Roberts smiled, the tight-jawed smile of a fighter.

"It's a case of pull, then; a pull as though Satan himself were just behind and in hot pursuit. Things are bound to give if one pulls hard enough."

Armstrong's face returned to the grate. His slippered feet spread wider than before.

"I'm not much good at pulling," he commented.

Roberts sat a moment in silence.

"I repeat, if I can be of any assistance—" he commented. "No butting in, you understand."

"Yes, I understand, and thank you sincerely. I doubt if you can help any though—if any one can. It's the old complaint mostly."

"Publishers who fail to appreciate, I gather."

"Partly."

"And what more, may I ask?"

Armstrong stretched back listlessly, his eyes half closed.

"Everything, it seems, to me to-night, every cursed thing!" Restless in spite of his seeming inertia he straightened nervously. His fingers, slender almost as those of a woman, opened and closed intermittently. "First of all, the manuscript of my new book came back this morning, the one I've been working on for the last year. The expressman delivered it just after you left. That started the day wrong. Then came a succession of little things. Breakfast, with coffee stone-cold, and soggy rolls; I couldn't swallow a mouthful.

Afterward I cut myself shaving, and I was late for lecture, and there was no styptic in the house, and I got down to my class with a collar looking as though I'd had my throat cut. The lecture room was chilly, beastly chilly, and about half the men had colds. Every twentieth word I'd say some one would sneeze and interrupt. On top of this one chap on the front row had neglected to complete his toilet and sat there for half an hour manicuring his nails, every blessed one of the ten; I counted them, while I was trying to explain proximal principles. At noon we had some more of that abominable soup with carrots in it. Carrots! I detest the name and the whole family; and we've had them every day now for a week. After lunch another big thing. I'd applied for position as lecturer in the summer school, applied early. The president met me to-day and remarked casually, very casually, that the man for the place had already been selected. He was very sorry of course, but—Back at the department I found that Elrod, one of my assistants, was sick, and of necessity I had to take his place in the laboratory. Inside half an hour some bumpkin dropped an eight-ounce bottle of sulphuretted hydrogen. It spattered everywhere—and the smell! I feel like holding my nose yet. Later the water got stopped up, and for love or money no plumber—" The speaker paused, his shoulders lifted eloquently. "But what's the use of itemizing. It's been the same all day long, one petty rasp after another. To cap the climax Elice is out of town. She's got an English class in a high-school in a dinky little burg out about twenty miles and goes out there every Thursday. I forgot this was the day until I pulled the knocker. That's all, I guess, except that I'm here."

Roberts smiled, the deliberate smile of tolerant understanding.

"One of those days, wasn't it," he commented sympathetically.

"Yes," shortly, "and it seems lately as though that was the only kind I had—seems as though it was not one but an endless succession.... It's all so petty, so confoundedly petty and irritating, and the outlook for the future seems so similar." Of a sudden the speaker arose, selected a bit of rice paper from the mantel, and began rolling a cigarette swiftly. The labor complete he paused, the little white cylinder between his fingers. A moment he stood so, irresolute or intentionally deliberate; without apology or comment he poured a second glass of liquor even full from the red decanter and drank it in silence. "On the square, Darley," he blazed, "I expected a lot from that last book, banked on it; and it's gone flat, like the others." He resumed his seat and the cigarette flamed. "I worked hard on it, did my level best. I don't believe I can ever do any better—and now it's failed miserably. It knocks my pins clean out from under me."

For a time the room was quiet. Roberts did not smile this time, or offer sympathy. The occasion for that had gone by. He merely waited in the fulness of knowledge, until the first hot flood of resentment had cooled, until the inevitable reaction that followed was on. Deliberate, direct to the point, he struck.

"You're satisfied I'm your friend, are you?" he asked abruptly.

The other looked his surprise.

"Emphatically, yes. One of the few I have—it seems to-night."

"And I couldn't possibly have any selfish motive in—in tearing you loose from your moorings?"

"None whatever that I can imagine. Why?"

"You won't take offence either if I advise plainly?"

"No, I'm not a fool—yet. What is it, Darley,—your advice?"

Again Roberts paused, deliberately now, unemotionally.

"My advice then is to chuck it, for to-day and to-morrow and all time: the University, this whole artistic rainbow, chuck it as though it were hot, red hot, and get down to earth. Is that brutally plain enough?"

Unconsciously Armstrong had sat up, expectant. A moment he remained so, taking in the thought, all its implications, its suddenly suggested possibilities; as the full revolutionary significance of the idea came home of a sudden he dropped back in his place. With an effort he smiled.

"To answer your question: yes, I think that is brutally frank enough," he said. A moment longer he remained quiet, thinking, the idea expanding. "Chuck it," he repeated half to himself. "It sounds sensible certainly, to-night particularly." New thoughts came, thoughts like the sifting of dead ashes. "Chuck it," feverishly, "and admit incompetency, cowardice, failure absolute!" For the third time he was on his feet. "No, never. I'll go to the devil first." His fingers were on the red decanter, his brown eyes aflame. "I'll—"

"Armstrong!"

No answer, although the fingers halted.

"Steve!"

Still no answer; but bit by bit the hand retreated.

"Steve," repeated, "sit down, please; please, I say. Let's talk this matter over a little rationally. People have changed their minds before, some few billions of them—and made good afterward too. Have a little patience, man, and sit down. I have a proposition to make to you."

Reluctantly Armstrong obeyed. His face was still unnaturally pale and he was breathing hard, but he obeyed. Back in his seat he waited a second, uncertain; with an effort he faced his companion fairly.

"I—realize I'm an ass, Darley," he began, hesitantly, "and that this sort of thing is melodramatically cheap." The white had left his face now and words were coming more easily. "I won't attempt to apologize, I just simply admit the truth. I've lost my grip this evening."

"Forget it." The voice was commonplace. "Just forget it."

"I can't; I'm not built that way; but I wish you would. If there's one thing I hate more than another it's cheap heroics."

"I know it—and understand. Let it go at that."

"Thank you. All right." It was matter of fact, but such with an effort. "Let's hear your proposition."

As usual Roberts wasted no preface.

"The suggestion is merely in line with what I said before. In so many words, it's to throw up this place of yours in the University and get into business. You'll come into contact with realities that way and realities are eternally opposed to—cobwebs. You'll be happier and more contented, I'm positive, once you get adjusted." He gave his listener a keen look. "I've got an opening in mind right now. Say the word and I'll have the place ready for you the day they appoint your successor in the University. Do you care to consider it?"

"Consider, yes, certainly." Armstrong had lit a pipe and puffed at it shortly. "It's white of you too to offer it. I know it's a good thing or you wouldn't make the suggestion."

"It's not as good as Graham's offer," refuted the other evenly, "places like that don't dangle loose every day; but it will pay you better than a university chair, and it offers possibilities—you anticipate probably,—it's in connection with the new electric line. Between ourselves, Armstrong, this system is going to be a big thing when it's complete. This is a straight tip. I happen to be in a position to know. I also happen to be in position to put you very near the basement, providing you wish to come in with us unhampered." The voice halted meaningly. "That's all I'm at liberty to say now, until you are really in and prove unmistakably—I'll have several things more to tell you then."

"Don't misunderstand me, Darley," he said slowly, "or take offence, please; but—but, to scrape off the veneer, you don't trust me very far even yet, do you?"

There was a moment of silence, time for second thought.

"I can't misunderstand what you mean," said Roberts; "but unfortunately there are others besides yourself for me to consider." The voice was patient, unnaturally so. "I've already talked more than I should."

"If I accepted," unobservant, Armstrong's mind was running on in its own channel, "the place you mean would take my entire time. In a way it would be like Graham's offer. I'd be compelled—you catch the idea, don't you?"

"Yes." This time the other did not amplify.

"You know why I refused that proposition before. We beat the brush pretty thoroughly at that time." It was declination involved, but declination nevertheless unmistakable. "It's a rocky road I'm on, and with occasional mudholes such as—well—such as I fell into to-night; but somehow I can't leave it. I won't try to defend it this time. I'm not in the mood. But when it comes to breaking free, taking a new trail—I simply can't do it, can't!"

"Very well." The voice was non-committal. Waiting, Armstrong thought there would be more to follow, a comment at least; but there was none. Roberts merely leaned back more comfortably in his place, remained so for a minute while like smoke the former subject faded from the horizon. Armstrong grew conscious that he was being observed intently.

"By the way," introduced Roberts, abruptly, "I've decided to give up my residence here in the suburbs. They're remodelling the office building I'm in, you know: adding another floor, an elevator, and one thing and another. I've rented a suite in the addition, to be fitted out after some ideas of my own. They'll begin on it inside a week."

For a moment Armstrong said nothing.

"I'm not particularly surprised," he commented at last, "that is, not surprised that you're going to quit me. It was merely a question of time until this place we're living in here got too small for you. When will you go?"

"The lease gives them a month to deliver."

"A month. All right." There was frost forming in the tone. "I'll try and lassoo another mate in that time. The place isn't particularly pretentious, but, nevertheless, I can't afford to inhabit it alone." He smiled, but it was not his customary companionable smile. "You're on the incline and trudging up steadily, aren't you, old man?"

For an instant Roberts returned the look with the analytic one Armstrong knew so well.

"I trust so," he returned. A pause, again sufficient for second thought. "Looking into the immediate future I see a lot of grinding to be done, and I need machinery to do it with. This down town move is merely part of the campaign."

"I see," Armstrong ignored the explanation, even perverted it intentionally. "And the next installation of machinery will be in stone out on Nob Hill among the other imitation colonial factories. When's that to be, if I may ask?"

Roberts said nothing.

"When's it to be, Darley?" repeated Armstrong. "You have it in mind, haven't you?"

This time Roberts turned, his eyes unsmiling, his lips tight.

"When have I offended you, and how, Armstrong?" he countered directly. "Tell me that."

"Offended!" Roused out of his ill humor Armstrong flushed penitently. "You've never offended, never. On the contrary, you're only too patient with my tantrums." He jerked himself together impulsively. "I didn't mean anything by that at all. I'm blooming glad to see you prosper. I always knew you would."

"The imitation colonial—factory then—" Roberts recalled slowly.

"Just a dream, a fancy, an air castle."

"No, a reality—I hope."

"What?—a miracle! But how about the tape line?"

"I repeat: I hope. Hope always refers to the future—the indefinite future."

Armstrong smiled broadly, shrugged. Banter tingled on the tip of his tongue, but for some reason remained unspoken. Abruptly as it had arisen the subject vanished beneath the surface. Merely the memory of that suggestion of things to come remained.

In the silence Roberts glanced at the clock and arose preparatory to bed. Watching the familiar action, a new thought sprang full-fledged to Armstrong's brain, a sudden appreciation of the unconscious dependence he had grown to feel on the other man. The thought took words.

"On the square, old man," he said soberly, "I hate to have you go. It'll be beastly lonely here without you to sit down on me and make me feel foolish." He gestured in mute eloquence. "It means the end between you and me the moment you pack your trunk. We may both put up a bluff—but just the same it's the end."

Roberts halted thoughtfully where he stood.

"The end? I wonder—and who will be to blame?"

"Neither of us," swiftly. "It was inevitable. We'll simply drift apart. You recall I prophesied once before—"

"Yes, I recall."

Armstrong started involuntarily. Another memory had intruded.

"You remember—something else I predicted, do you?"

A slow smile formed on Roberts' lips.

"You said that sometime we'd hate each other, in the same measure that we were friends now."

"Yes; and it's so. I feel it; why I don't know, can't imagine—yet. But it will come about as surely as to-morrow will come." He looked at his companion steadily, unsmilingly prophetic. "Good-bye, friend Darley Roberts. You're going—and you won't return. Good-bye."

An instant Roberts stood as he was, motionless; then he turned swiftly.

"You're morbid to-night, Armstrong," he returned slowly. "In the morning the sun will shine and the world will look very different. As for my leaving—you'll find another man who'll make a lot better mate than I am. I'm not a good fellow in the least."

"I know it," bluntly. "That's why you're good for me." Unconsciously his glance travelled to the mantel, and shifted hurriedly. "I'm a kind of clinging vine, I guess. To change the figure of speech, I need a stiff rudder to keep me headed straight to windward. I'll—miss you," simply.

Roberts hesitated a moment, choosing his words carefully.

"We can't very well always be together, though," he suggested at last slowly.

"No, we can't. I realize it. It's—Pardon an ass and go to bed, old man."

For perhaps half a minute Roberts stood there, the fire from the open grate lighting his face, his big capable hands loose at his sides. He made no motion to leave, nor for a space to speak; characteristically abrupt, he turned, facing his companion directly.

"Armstrong," he said, "I can't work up to things delicately and have them seemingly happen by chance. Nature didn't endow me with that ability. I have to come out with a broadside shot or not at all. I'm going to do so now. Why don't you get married? Miss Gleason will be a better rudder immeasurably than I am."

Involuntarily Armstrong flushed, slowly the color faded. He said nothing.

"I know I'm intruding and offending," went on the other; "you show that, but you said a bit ago I was your friend and the thing is on my mind. Believe this at least: I was never more your friend than when I advise the move now. I repeat: why don't you get married, at once?"

"Why? You know why, Darley. It's the old reason—the butcher, the baker, and the candlestick maker. They still hold the fort."

"No, not for you—unless you let them. Forgive another broadside. If you get pinched temporarily let a friend be of service. I'm not afraid to trust you. Anyway I chance it. We all have to chance something for happiness. Don't delay any longer, man, don't!"

"Don't?" Of a sudden Armstrong glanced up and met the other's look steadily. "Don't?" he repeated. "Why do you say that, please?"

A second Roberts met the lifted questioning eyes.

"Because I meant it," he said. "Please don't ask me to say more."

"But I do ask it," pressed Armstrong, stubbornly. "You meant something particular by that, something I have the right to know."

"Won't you consider what I suggested," asked Roberts in a low tone; "merely consider it?"

"Perhaps after you tell me what you meant. Why 'don't,' please?"

On the cosy room fell silence, — the silence of midnight; the longest silence of that interrupted understanding. For a long while Roberts stood precisely as he was; he started walking, measuring the breadth of the room and back again; something the watcher had never known him to do before, never in the years of acquaintance, no matter what the uncertainty or difficulty confronting. A second time he followed the trail back and forth, until, watching him, the spectator felt at last something like terror of the thing he had deliberately conjured and that now was inevitably coming very near; for at last Roberts had halted, was standing over him.

"In all the time that I've known you, Armstrong," said a voice, a new voice, "you've asked my advice repeatedly, asked the reason for it, insisted that I explain minutely, and disregarded it absolutely. I've tried to be honest with you each time, tried to be of service; and still you've disregarded. It's been the same to-night, the old, old story. I've been dead in earnest, tried to be unselfish, and still you question and doubt and insist." A second the voice halted, the speaker glancing down, not analytically or whimsically, as usual, but of a sudden icy cold. "You insist now, against my request, and once more I'm going to humor you. You wish to know what I meant by 'don't' delay. I meant just this, man, just this and no more: Chances for happiness come to us all sometime in our lives. They knock at our door and wait for us to open. Sometimes, not often, they knock twice; but they don't keep on knocking forever. There are a multitude of other doors in the world and, after a while, opportunity, our opportunity, goes by, and never returns; no matter how loudly we call. Is that clear enough, man?"

"In the abstract, yes." Armstrong's lips were dry and he moistened them unconsciously. "In the concrete, though, as it applies to my — happiness — "

"God, you're an egotist, Armstrong! Is it possible you can't understand, or won't?"

Slowly, with an effort, Armstrong arose; his face of a sudden gray, his hands fastened to the back of his chair.

"You mean to suggest that Elice," he began, "that Elice — You dare to suggest that to me?"

"Dare?"

They looked at each other, not three feet apart.

"Dare?" Roberts repeated.

"Darley!"

"Don't! I've argued, advised, used persuasion — everything. Take that as a warning if you wish, or disregard it if you choose. I'm done."

On the chair back the fingers locked tighter and tighter, until they grew white. Tardy comprehension was coming at last.

"You mean to warn me," Armstrong scarcely recognized his own voice, "that you yourself — "

"Yes, I myself. That's why I warned you."

"You yourself," he repeated, "whom I introduced and took with me as my friend, my best friend — you — Judas!"

"Re-introduced." Roberts' eyes were as steady as his voice. "Re-introduced — mark that. Miss Gleason has forgotten, but she was the first girl I met in the University, when I had one suit of frayed clothes to my name, and my stock was below par. Miss Gleason has forgotten, I say, had no reason to remember; but I — Nor — Judas; drop that for all time.... I've warned you, you understand."

"Darley!"

"No — Roberts. I'm no hypocrite. You've precipitated this understanding, compelled it; but perhaps it's as well. I'll move out of here to-morrow instead of in a month, if you wish. Do you wish it?"

Bit by bit the hands on the chair back, that had been so tense, loosened, and Armstrong sank back in his seat, his face turned away.

"I don't know — yet." His fingers were twitching aimlessly. "I want to think.... You, of all men, you!" He turned, his eyes ablaze, his voice thick. "Yes, go to-morrow, damn you! and as for your warning, do as you please, get between us if you can." He laughed raspingly. "I'll delay — dangle, you catch that — as long as I see fit. I dare you."

An instant Roberts stood as he was; slowly and without a word he started for his room. As he did so Armstrong arose swiftly and, all but gropingly, his hand sought the red decanter on the mantel. "I dare you," he repeated blindly, "dare you!"

"Armstrong!" Roberts had halted, looking back. "Not for any one's sake but your own — think a second, man."

"To hell with you and thought!"

Without a sound this time or another glance the door to Roberts' room opened and closed and Armstrong was alone.

CHAPTER VI

A WARNING

With a dexterity born of experience Harry Randall looked up from his labor of separating the zone of carbon from the smaller segment of chop that had escaped the ravages of a superheated frying-pan and smiled across the table at his wife.

"On the contrary," he said, refuting a pessimistic observation previously made by the person addressed, "I think you're doing fine. I can see a distinct improvement every month. On the whole you're really becoming an admirable cook."

"Undoubtedly!" The voice dripped with irony. "That very chop, for instance—"

"Is merely a case in point," amiably. "Some people, unscientific people, might contend that it was overdone; but the initiated—that's us—know better. Meat, particularly from the genus hog, should always be well cooked. It obviates the possibility of trichina infection absolutely."

"And those biscuits," equivocally. "I'll wager they'd sink like steel billets."

Her husband inspected the articles designated with a judicial eye.

"Better so. We're thus saved the temptation of eating them. All statistics prove that hot biscuits and dyspepsia—"

"The salad, then," wearily.

"Hygienic beyond a doubt. The superabundance of seasoning to which you doubtless refer may be unusual; nevertheless, it's a leaning in the right direction. Condiments of all kinds tend to stimulate the flow of the gastric juice; and that, you know, from your physiology, is what does the digestive business."

Margery Randall laughed, against her will.

"And last of all the coffee," she suggested.

"Frankly, as coffee, it is a little peculiar; but considered as hot water merely, it leaves nothing to be desired; and science teaches again that, like condiments, hot water—"

The two laughed together; temporarily the atmosphere cleared.

"Seriously, Harry," asked the girl, "do you really think I'll ever get so I can cook things that aren't an insult?" She swept the indigestible repast between them with a hopeless look. "I'm trying my best, but at times like this I get discouraged."

"Certainly you will," with conviction. "Now this bread, for instance," he held up a slice to illustrate, "is as good as any one can make."

"And unfortunately was one of the few things that I didn't make. It's bakery bread, of course, silly."

Randall dropped the offending staff of life as though it were hot.

"These cookies, then." He munched one with the pleasure of an epicure. "They're good thoroughly."

"Elice Gleason baked them for me to-day," icily. "She was here all the afternoon."

An instant of silence followed; glancing half sheepishly across the board Randall saw something that made him arise from his seat abruptly.

"Margery, little girl," his arms were around her. "Don't take it so seriously. It's all a joke, honest." With practised skill he kissed away the two big tears that were rapidly gathering. "Of course you'll learn; every one has to have practice; and it's something you never did before, something entirely new."

"That's just the point," repeated the girl. The suddenly aroused tears had ceased to flow, but she still looked the image of despondency. "It's something I've never had to do, and I'll never learn. I've been trying for practically a year now and things get worse and worse."

"Not worse," hopefully; "you merely think so. You're just a bit discouraged and tired to-night—that's all."

"I know it and, besides, I can't help it." She was winking hard again against two fresh tears. "I spoiled two cakes this afternoon. Elice tried to show me how to make them; and I burned my finger"—she held up a swaddled member for inspection—"horribly. I just can't do this housework, Harry, just simply can't."

"Yes, you can." Once more the two teary recruits vanished by the former method. "You can do anything."

The girl shook her head with a determination premeditated.

"No; I repeat that I've tried, and it's been a miserable failure. I—think we'll have to have the maid back again, for good."

"The maid!" Randall laughed, but not so spontaneously as was normal. "We don't want a maid bothering around, Margery. We want to be alone." He had a brilliant thought, speedily reduced to action. "How could I treat injured fingers like this properly if there was a maid about?"

"There wouldn't be any burned fingers then," refuted the girl. Intentionally avoiding the other's look, she arose from the neglected dinner-table decisively and, the man following slowly, led the way to the living-room. "Joking aside," she continued as she dropped into a convenient seat, "I mean it, seriously. I've felt this way for a long time, and to-day has been the climax. I simply won't spend my life cooking and dusting and—and washing dishes. Life's too short."

From out the depths of the big davenport Harry Randall inspected steadily the rebellious little woman opposite. He did not answer at once, it was not his way; but he was thinking seriously. To say that the present moment was a surprise would be false. For long, straws had indicated the trend of the wind, and he was not blind. There was an excuse for the attitude, too. He was just enough to realize that. As she had said, she was born differently, bred differently, educated to a life of ease. And he, Harry Randall, had known it from the first, knew it when he married her. Just now, to be sure, he was financially flat, several months ahead of his meagre salary; but that did not alter the original premise, the original obligation. He remembered this now as he looked at her, remembered and decided—the only way it seemed to him possible an honorable man could decide.

"Very well, Margery," he said gravely, "you may have the maid back, of course, if you wish it. I had hoped we might get along for a time, while we were paying for the things in the house, anyway; but"—he looked away—"I guess we'll manage it somehow."

"Somehow!" Margery glanced at him with only partial comprehension. "Is it really as bad as that, as hopeless?"

Randall smiled the slow smile that made his smooth face seem fairly boyish.

"I don't know exactly what you mean by bad, or hopeless; but it's a fact that so far we've been spending a good deal more than my income."

"I'm sorry, dear, really." It was the contrition of one absolutely unaccustomed to consideration of ways and means, uncomprehending. "Particularly so just now with winter coming on and—and girls, you know, have to get such a lot of things for winter."

This time Randall did not smile; neither did he show irritation.

"What, for instance?" he inquired directly.

"Oh, a tailored suit for one thing, and a winter hat, and high shoes, and—and a lot of things."

"Do you really need them, Margery?" It was prosaic pathos, but pathos nevertheless. "There's coal to be bought, you know, and my life insurance comes due next month. I don't want to seem to be stingy, you know that; but—" he halted miserably.

"Need them!" It was mild vexation. "Of course I need them, silly. A girl can't go around when the thermometer's below zero with net shirtwaists and open-work stockings."

"Of course," quickly. With an effort the smile returned. "Order what you need. I'll take care of that too"—he was going to repeat "somehow," then caught himself—"as soon as I can," he substituted.

The girl looked at him smilingly.

"Poor old Harry, henpecked Harry," she bantered gayly. Crossing over, her arms went around his neck. "Have an awful lot of troubles, don't you, professor man!"

The argument was irresistible and Randall capitulated.

"No, none whatever," he answered, as he was expected to answer; and once more sweet peace rested on the house of Randall.

Back in her place opposite once more Margery looked at her husband seriously, a pucker of perplexity on her smooth face.

"By the way," she digressed, "I've been wondering for some time now if anything's wrong with Elice and Steve. Has he hinted anything to you?"

"No; why?"

"Oh, I don't know anything definite; but he's been here three evenings the last week, you know, Sunday evening for one at that, and it looks queer."

"I've noticed it too," admitted Randall, "and he's coming again this evening. He asked permission and I couldn't well refuse. Not that I don't like to have him come," quickly, "but it interferes with my lectures next morning."

"And with our own evenings. I—just wish he wouldn't come so often."

Randall said nothing, but unconsciously he was stroking the bald spot already appearing on the crown of his head in a way he had when worried.

"And, besides," justified Margery, "it isn't treating Elice right. I think it's a shame."

This time the man looked up.

"She didn't say anything, intimate anything, I hope?" he hesitated.

"Of course not. It isn't her way. She's—queer for a woman, Elice is; she never gets confidential, no matter how good an opportunity you offer." A pause followed that spoke volumes. "Agnes Simpson, though, says there is something the matter—with Steve at least. They're talking about it in the department."

"Talking about what, Margery?" soberly. "He's a friend of ours, you know."

"Yes, I know," the voice was swift with a pent-up secret, "and we've tried hard to be nice to him; but, after all, we're not to blame that he—drinks!"

"Margery!" It was open disapproval this time, a thing unusual for Harry Randall. "We mustn't listen to such gossip, either of us. Steve and I have been chums for years and years and—we simply mustn't listen to such things at all."

For an instant the girl was silent; then the brown head tossed rebelliously.

"Well, I can't help it if people talk; and it isn't fair of you to suppose that I pass it on either—except to you. You know that I—" she checked herself. "It isn't as though Agnes was the only one either," she defended. "I've heard it several times lately." Inspiration came and she looked at her husband directly. "Honest, Harry, haven't you heard it too?"

The man hesitated, and on the instant solid ground vanished from beneath his feet.

"Yes, I have," he admitted weakly. "It's a burning shame too that people will concoct—" He halted suddenly, listening. His eyes went to the clock. "I had no idea it was so late," he digressed as the bell rang loudly. "That's Steve now. I know his ring."

Alone in the up-stairs study, which with its folding-bed was likewise spare sleeping-room and again smoking-room,—Margery had not yet surrendered to the indiscriminate presence of tobacco smoke, — Steve Armstrong ignored the chair Randall had proffered and remained standing, his hands deep in his trousers' pockets, a look new to his friend—one restless, akin to reckless—on his usually good-humored face. Contrary again to precedent his dress was noticeably untidy, an impression accentuated by a two-days' growth of beard and by neglected linen. That something far from normal was about to transpire Randall knew at a glance, but courteously seemed not to notice. Instead, with a familiar wave, he indicated the cigar-jar he kept on purpose for visitors and took a pipe himself.

"I haven't had my after-dinner smoke yet," he commented. "Better light up with me. It always tastes better when one has company."

"Thanks." Armstrong made a selection absently and struck a match; but, the unlighted cigar in his fingers, let the match burn dead. "I don't intend to bother you long," he plunged without preface. "I know you want to work." He glanced nervously at the door to see that it was closed. "I just wanted to have a little talk with you, a— little heart-to-heart talk."

"Yes." Randall's face showed no surprise, but his pipe bowl was aglow and his free hand was caressing his bald spot steadily.

"Frankly, old man," the other had fallen back into his former position, his hands concealed, his attitude stiffly erect, "I'm in the deuce of a frame of mind to-night—and undecided." He laughed shortly. "You're the remedy that occurred to me."

"Yes," Randall repeated, this time with the slow smile, "I am a sort of remedy. Sit down and tell me about it. I'm receptive at least."

"Sit down! I can't, Harry." The restless look became one of positive repugnance. "I haven't been able to for a half-hour at a stretch for a week."

"Try it anyway," bluntly. "It won't do you any harm to try."

"Nor any good either. I know." He threw himself into a seat with a nervous scowl upon his face. "I haven't been able to do any real work for an age, which is worse," he continued. "My lectures lately have been a disgrace to the college. No one knows it better than myself."

A moment Randall hesitated, but even yet he did not put an inquiry direct.

"Yes?" he suggested again.

"I'm stale, I guess, or have lost my nerve or—or something." Armstrong smiled,—a crooked smile that failed to extinguish the furrows on his forehead. "By the way, have you got a little superfluous nerve lying about that you could stake me with?"

Randall echoed the laugh, because it seemed the only possible answer, but that was all.

In the silence that followed Armstrong looked at his friend opposite, the nervous furrow between his eyes deepening.

"I suppose you're wondering," he began at last, "just what's the matter with me and what I want of you. Concerning the first, there's a lot I might say, but I won't; I'll spare you. As to what I want to ask of you—Frankly, Harry, straight to the point and conventional reticence aside, ought I to marry or oughtn't I?" He caught the other's expression and answered it quickly. "I know this is a peculiar thing to ask and seems, looking at it from some angles, something I shouldn't ask; but you know all the circumstances between Elice and me and, in a way, our positions are a good deal similar. Just what do you think? Don't hesitate to tell me exactly."

In his seat Randall shifted uncomfortably; to gain time he filled his pipe afresh,—a distinct dissipation for the man of routine that he was.

"Frankly, as you suggest, Steve," he answered finally, "I'd rather not discuss the subject, rather not advise. It's—you know why—so big and personal."

"I realize that and have apologized already for bringing it up; but I can't decide myself—I've tried; and Elice—there are reasons why she can't assist now either. It's—" he made a motion to rise, but checked himself—"it's something that has to be decided now too."

"Has to?" Randall's eyes behind the big lens of his glasses were suddenly keen. "Why, Steve?"

"Because it's now or never," swiftly. "I've—we've hesitated until we can't delay any longer. I'm not sure that it's not been too long already, that's why Elice can't figure." He drew himself up with an effort, held himself still. "We've crossed the dividing line, Elice and I, and we're drifting apart. Just how the thing has come about I don't know; but it's true. We're on different roads somehow and we're getting farther apart every month." He sprang to his feet, his face turned away. "Soon—It's simply hell, Harry!"

Randall sat still; recollecting, he laughed,—a laugh that he tried to make natural.

"Oh, pshaw!" He laughed again. "You're mixing up some of the novels you're writing with real life. This sort of thing is nonsense, pure nonsense."

"No, it's so," flatly. "I've tried hard enough to think it different, but I couldn't because it is so. It's hell, I say!"

"Don't you love her, man?" abruptly.

"Love her!" Armstrong wheeled, his face almost fierce. "Of course I love her. A hundred times yes. I'm a cursed fool over her."

"Sit down then and tell me just what's on your mind. You're magnifying a mole-hill of some kind into a snow-capped peak. Sit down, please. You—irritate me that way."

A second Armstrong hesitated. His face a bit flushed, he obeyed.

"That's better." The brusqueness was deliberately intentional. "Now out with it, clear the atmosphere. I'm listening."

Armstrong looked at his friend a bit suspiciously; but the mood was too strong upon him to cease now even if he would.

"Just what do you wish to know?" he asked in tentative prelude. "Give me a clew."

"What you wish to tell me," evenly. "Neither more nor less."

"You have no curiosity?"

Randall made no comment this time, merely waited.

"Very well, then, if you have no curiosity.... I don't know how much to tell you anyway, what you don't already know. As I said when I first came in, I didn't have it in mind to bore you at all, I just wanted to ask your opinion—" The speaker halted and hurriedly lit the cigar he had been holding. "To jump into the thick of it, I got a little letter from the president to-day, a little—warning." Armstrong smoked fiercely until the flame lit up his face. "It's the bitterest humiliation of my life, Harry, the last straw!"

CHAPTER VII

REBELLION

For a moment Harry Randall said nothing, then deliberately he glanced up and met his friend's eyes direct.

"Begin at the beginning and tell me the whole story," he said soberly. "I had no idea the thing was really so serious."

"Well, it is, take that for granted. It's likely to be the end, so far as I am concerned."

"Cut that out, Steve," shortly. "It's melodramatic and cheap. Things can't be so bad if we look at them sanely." He hesitated, and went on with distinct effort. "To begin with, I'm going to ask you a question. I hate it, you know that without my telling you, but things have gone too far to mince matters evidently. I've heard a number of times lately that you were drinking. Is it so?"

"Who told you that?" hotly.

"Never mind who. I tell you I never believed a word of it until you mentioned the president's warning. Now—Is it so?"

Armstrong's face went red,—red to the roots of his hair,—then slowly shaded white until it was ghastly pale.

"Yes; it's useless, it seems, to deny it. That others knew, were talking about it, though—It's true, Harry. I admit it."

Slowly, slowly, Randall knocked the ashes out of the pipe-bowl and put it away in a drawer of the table.

"Very well, Steve. I shan't moralize. None of us men are so good we can afford to begin throwing stones.... Let's go back a bit to the beginning. There must be one somewhere, a cause. Just what's the trouble, old man?"

"Trouble!" It was the spark to tinder, the lead at last. "Everything, Harry, everything." A halt for composure. "I suppose if I were to pick out one single thing, though, that was worse than another, it's my writing. I think, I know, that's what brought on the whole cursed mess. Until my last book failed I had hope and the sun shone. When that went down—down like a lump of lead—I haven't been able to do a thing, care for a thing since. My brain simply quit work too. It died, and the best of me died with it."

"And you began to drink."

"Yes, like a fish. Why not, since I was dead and it helped me to forget?"

"Steve! I hate to preach, it doesn't become me; but—"

"Preach if you want to; you can't hurt my feelings now." Armstrong grew calm, for the first time that evening. "When a fellow has worked as I have worked for years, and hoped against hope, and still hoped on and worked on after failure and failure and failure three times repeated—No, don't worry about hurting my feelings, Harry. Say what you please."

"I wasn't going to hurt your feelings," evenly; "I was only going to preach a little. I merely wanted to take exception to that forgetting business. If you'll just hold hard for a bit you'll forget normally, not artificially. Another six months and you'll be hard at another scheme, developing it; and the way you feel now—It'll be a joke then, a sort of nightmare to laugh over."

"Never.... Don't get restless; I'm not irresponsible now. I'm merely telling you. I've been asleep and dreaming for a long time, but at last I'm awake. Come what may, and truly as I'm telling you now, I'll never write another novel. I couldn't if I wanted to—I've tried and know; and I wouldn't if I could. There's a limit to everything, and the limit of my patience and endurance is reached. I'm done for now and for all time." The voice was not excited now or unnaturally tense, but normal, almost conversational.

"For ten years I've fought the good fight. Every spare hour of that time that I could muster I've worked. I've lain awake night after night and night after night tossing and planning and struggling for a definite end. The thing got to be a sort of religion to me. I convinced myself that it was my work in the big scheme, my allotted task, and I tried faithfully to do it. I never spared myself. I dissected others, of course; but I dissected myself most, clear to the bone. I even took a sort of joy in it when it hurt most, for I felt it was my contribution and big. I'm not bragging now, mind. I'm merely telling you as it was. I've gone on doing this for ten years, I say. When I failed again I tried harder still. I still believed in myself—and others. Recognition, appreciation, might be delayed, but eventually it would come, it must; for this was my work,—to please others, to amuse them, to carry them temporarily out of the rut of their work-a-day lives and make them forget. I believed this, I say, believed and hoped and waited and worked on until the last few months. Then—I told you what happened. Then—" For the first time the speaker paused. He shrugged characteristically. "But what's the use of disturbing the corpse. I've simply misread the signs in the sky—that's all. I couldn't produce a better novel than I've written if I had the longevity of the Wandering Jew and wrote to the end—for I've done my best. The great public that I've torn myself to pieces to please has seen the offering and passed it by. They will have none of it—and they're the arbiters." He shrugged again, the narrow shoulders eloquent. "So be it. I accept; but I offer no more. For all time, to finality, I'm done, done!"

"Even if some of your books should win?"

"If every one of them should do so. If half a dozen publishers came to me personally and begged me to resume work. I may be a poor artist, may lack completely the artistic subservience to or superiority to discouragement, probably I do; but at least I know I'm human. I'm like a well in the desert that's been pumped empty and left never a mark on the surrounding sand. I couldn't produce again if I wanted to; I'm drained dry."

Randall said nothing. He knew this other man.

"I tell you I'm awake, Harry, at last, and see things as they are; things now so childishly obvious that it seems incredible I could have gone on so long without recognizing them. People prate about appreciation of artists of various kinds and of their work, grow maudlin over it by artificial light in the small hours of the night. And how do they demonstrate it? Once in a while, the isolated exception that proves the rule, by recognizing and rewarding the genius in his lifetime. Once in a very, very long time, I say. Mind, I don't elevate myself as a genius. I'm merely speaking as an observer who's awakened and knows. As a rule what do they do? Let him struggle and work and eat his heart out in obscurity and without recognition. Let him starve himself body and soul. After he's dead, after a year or a hundred years, after there is no possibility of his receiving the reward or the inspiration, they arouse. His fame spreads. His name becomes a household word. They desecrate his grave, if they can find it, by hanging laurel on his tombstone. They tear the wall-paper from the house where he once chanced to live into ribbons for souvenirs. If he happens to be a painter the picture that brought him enough perhaps to keep body and soul together for a month is fought for until eventually it sells for a fortune. If he was a writer they bid for a scrap of his manuscript more than he received for his whole work. There are exceptions, I say; but even exceptions only prove the rule. Think over the names of the big artists, the big geniuses. How many of them are alive or were appreciated in their own lives? How many living to-day compare in the public appreciation with those dead? None of them, practically, none. And still do you or does any other sane person fancy that human beings are degenerating every generation, that artistic genius is decadent? It's preposterous, unthinkable! It merely points the moral that history repeats itself. Some place, somewhere, the greatest artist in the world is painting the greatest picture the world has ever known—and this same world passes him by. It must be so, for human beings advance with every generation inevitably. Some place, somewhere, the biggest writer of all time is writing the biggest book—and his neighbors smile because his clothes are rusty. This is the reward they get in their own day and their own generation, when it would sweeten their lives, make them worth living. The fellow who invents a mouse-trap or a safety razor or devises a way of sticking two hogs where one was killed before, inherits the earth, sees his name and fame heralded in every periodical; while the other, the real man—God, it's unbelievable, neither more nor less; and still it's true to the last detail. Again, it's all civilization, the civilization we brag of; magnificent twentieth century civilization!"

Still Randall said nothing, still waited.

Armstrong hesitated, drumming on the arm of his chair with his slender fingers. But the lull was only temporary, the storm not past; the end was not yet.

"I suppose," he forged on, "the work should be its own reward, its own justification. At least would-be artists are told so repeatedly. Whenever one rebels at the injustice the world is there with this sophistry, feeds him with it as a nurse feeds pap to a crying child, until he's full and temporarily comatose. But just suppose for an instant that the same argument were used in any other field of endeavor. Suppose, for instance, you told the prospector who'd spent years searching for and who'd finally found a gold mine that his reward should be in the mere knowledge of having found it, the feeling of elation that he had added to the sum total of the world's wealth, and that he should relinquish it intact as a public trust. Just preach this gospel, and how long would you escape the mad-house? Or the architect who designs and superintends the construction of a sky-scraper. Take him aside and argue with him that the artistic satisfaction of having conceived that great pile of stone and steel should repay him for his work, that to expect remuneration was sordid and disgusting. Do you think he'd sign a certificate to the effect that you were normal and sane? And still how is it with a writer in this the twentieth century,—century of enlightenment and of progress? First of all he must go through the formative period, which means years. Nothing, even genius, springs without preparation into full bloom. No matter how good the idea, how big the thought, it must be moulded by a mastery of technique and a proficiency that only experience can give. And meanwhile he must live. How? No matter. The suggestion is mundane. Let him settle that for himself. At last, perhaps, if he has the divine spark, he gets a hearing. We'll suppose he accomplishes his purpose,—pleases them, makes them think, or laugh, or forget temporarily, as the case may be. In a way he has made an opening and arrived. And yet, though an artist, he is, first of all, a human being, an animal. The animal part of him demands insistently the good things of life. If he is normal he wants a home and a family of his own; and wants that home as good as that of his neighbor who practises law or makes soda biscuits.

With this premise what do the public, who don't know him personally but whom he serves just the same, do? The only way they can show their appreciation tangibly is by buying his work; giving him encouragement, making it possible to live and to write more. I repeat I know this is all mundane and commonplace and unæsthetic, but it's reality. And do they give this encouragement, buy themselves, and let him make his tiny royalty which in turn enables him to live, pass an appreciation on to their friends and induce them to buy? In a fractional proportion of times, yes. In the main, John, whom the writer has worked a year, day and night, to reach, by chance meets his friend Charley. 'By the way,' he remarks, 'I picked up that novel of Blank's lately. It's good, all right, all right; kept me up half the night to finish it. I want you to read it, old man. It's just your style. No use to buy it, though,' he adds hurriedly. 'Drop in sometime and I'll lend it to you.' Of a sudden he remembers. 'Come to think of it, though, I believe just now it's lent to Phil—or was it Dick who took it. The story's a corker and they've both had it.' He thinks again hard and remembers. 'I have it now. Dick gave it to Sam; he told me so. Get it from him yourself. I know you'll like it.' And so the lending goes on so long as the covers hold together. Meanwhile the writer, away off somewhere waiting and hoping and watching the sale, in return for the pleasure he gives John and Charley and Phil and Dick and Sam and the rest, and in consideration of that year of work and weariness and struggle, gets enough perhaps to buy a meal at a Chinese restaurant. This is appreciation, I say, enlightened twentieth century appreciation; and the beauty of it is that every one of that company who get his work for nothing feel that by their praise and by reading his work they've given that writer, who can't possibly know anything about it, all that he could possibly desire." For the first time that evening Armstrong paused to laugh. "Oh, it's humorous, all right, when one stops to consider and appreciate! Just suppose, though, in the name of fair play, some one had suggested to John that he throw that copy of his in the furnace where no one could possibly borrow it, and then go on telling his appreciation. Just supposing some one had suggested that! Do you fancy John would have considered that person wholly sane? And still that writer, besides being an artist, is an animal with a stomach and needs a home to live in, and maybe is human enough to have burdened himself with a wife and—and children—"

"Steve, confound it, you've gone on long enough."

"I know it—too long."

"It doesn't do any good to rail at something you can't help, that no one can help."

"Admitted. I'm just talking to myself—and you. It's all the same."

"You've never starved yet or gone without clothes, so far as I know."

"Starved, no. I had soup at my boarding-house for lunch again to-day—soup with carrots in it. Hungry—I don't know. This is a big world we're in and I've never had the chance even to look over the horizon yet. Hungry? I've been hungry for—Elice for years, and I don't dare—Hunger is awfully near to starvation sometimes, friend Harry."

Harry Randall squirmed. He saw it coming—it!

"Oh, things will come all right if you'll be patient," he said—and halted himself for the trite optimism.

"Elice won't; for she's gone already while I've been patient—gone and left me hungry."

"Nonsense. Rot, plain rot!"

"No, reality, plain reality. She probably wouldn't admit it yet, not even to herself, maybe doesn't know it yet herself; but I know. It's been coming on a long time. I see it all now."

Randall made a wry face. That was all.

"Yes, it's true, Harry, God's truth. I asked you a peculiar question a while ago,—asked whether I ought to marry. I didn't mean it; I was just maudlin. I know without asking that I mustn't. Even if Elice would consent—and I think she would consent yet, she's game—I mustn't. I'm waking up more all the time."

"Steve, you're maddening—impossible. I tell you, Elice will never change. You know it without my telling you."

"Yes, I know. It's I who have changed." He remembered suddenly. "Yes; it's I who have changed," he repeated slowly.

"Well, you'll change back again then." The effort to be severe and commonplace was becoming cumulatively difficult. "You must."

"Must change back—and marry Elice?"

"Yes," desperately.

"No, not if by a miracle I could change back."

"Why? For heaven's sake, why? Don't be a fool, man."

"Why?" without heat. "Do you really wish to know why?"

"Yes."

Armstrong deliberated.

"You yourself are one reason, friend Harry."

"I—I don't understand."

"Yes, you do. I'm not without observation. You yourself wouldn't advise me to marry now."

"Steve!"

"You wouldn't, and you know you wouldn't. No offence. We're simply looking things squarely in the eye. It's merely the tragedy of pennies among evolved humans who require dollars to live—and must live. Am I not right, friend of mine?"

No severity this time, no commonplace—nothing.

"I repeat, no offence; just square in the eye. Am I not right?"

"Right? I don't know. I can't answer." A sudden blaze. "You have no right to suggest—"

"No. Pardon me." Armstrong's face worked in spite of himself. "Forget that I did suggest, Harry. It was brutal of me."

Randall said nothing.

"But with Elice and myself it's different. I've awakened in time. Providence, perhaps, sometimes when we least expect it—"

"Steve!" Randall had glanced up quickly, self for the moment in abeyance. "What do you intend doing, tell me that?"

"Doing?" It was almost surprise. "Have you any honest doubt yet, after what I've told you?" He halted, scrutinizing his friend's face, and seemed satisfied. "I'm going to release her; release her unqualifiedly. I can at least be man enough to do that."

"And if you do—what of yourself?"

Armstrong smiled forcedly, a slow, mirthless smile. "Never mind about myself. I've glowed genially for a long time, tried after my own fashion to warm a hearth somewhere; but at last I'm burned out, nothing but cinders. Never mind about myself. The discussion is futile."

Randall hesitated; then he gestured impotently.

"Elice, then—For her sake at least—"

"It's for her sake I'll do it, because she'll never do it herself. I repeat, I can at least be man enough to do that much for her, make amends to that extent." He looked straight before him, seeing nothing. "She'll be happy yet, when I'm well out of the way."

"Steve!" Argument would not come, rebuttal; only that cry that acknowledged its own helplessness. "I can't bear to have things go that way. I know you both so well, like you so much."

"I realize that," dully; "but it's not your fault,—not any one's fault in particular that I can see."

Randall did not gesture this time. Even that avenue seemed barred.

"If I could only say something to influence you, to convince you—something adequate."

"There's nothing to be said that I can see, or done, for that matter. It's like a church catechism, cut and dried generations ahead."

It was the final word, and for a long time they sat there silent, unconscious of the passing minutes; alike gazing at the blank wall which circumstance had thrown in the way, alike looking for an opening where opening there was none. At last, when the silence had become unbearable, Randall roused, and with an effort forced a commonplace.

"Anyway, as yet you're reckoning without your host—in this case Elice," he formalized. "After you've seen her—"

"It will merely be ended then—that is all."

"I'm not so sure, even yet."

"I repeat that I know, know to finality. Some things one can't question when they're awake. Moreover, I have a reason for knowing."

It was a new note, that last comment; a note of repression where all before had been unrepressed. Moreover, it was a lead intentionally offered.

"What is it, Steve?" asked the other simply. "There's something yet which you haven't told me."

"Yes." Once more Armstrong's eyes were on the wall straight before him, the wall he did not see. "I merely suggested it a bit ago. I said Elice had drifted away while I was being patient. At first that drifting was very slow, so slow that I didn't realize it myself; during the last few months she's been going fast." The speaker moistened his lips unconsciously; but, watching, the other noticed. "Things seldom happen in this world without a reason, and they didn't in this case." Suddenly, without warning, he whirled, met the other eye to eye. "Do I need to suggest more?" he asked steadily.

"Suggest—more?" Randall's look was blank. "I don't believe I understand."

"I mean concerning—the reason I mentioned. Haven't you noticed anything yourself, had any intimation?"

"I know nothing, have noticed nothing."

"No?" Armstrong's scrutiny was merciless, all but incredulous. "Nothing concerning Elice and—and Darley Roberts—not a whisper?"

Against his will Randall's eyes dropped. At last he understood.

"You have heard. I thought so." Armstrong fumbled with his cuffs, played for time, which meant for self-control. "I'm glad. It saves my—explaining."

"Yes, I've heard." Randall's tongue lagged unwillingly. "I couldn't help it; but believed, in the least, before—no. I thought he was your friend."

"Was, yes. Now—It's been some time since we came to an understanding; and he told me, warned me. I don't blame him—or her. I've had my chance, ample chance, God knows.... It's simply true."

Randall looked up unbelievingly.

"And you don't hate him, you who were his friend?"

"Hate?... I don't know, don't know anything these days except that I'm down—down; down in the mire, deep!" It was the end, the last crumb of confidence, and Armstrong leaped to his feet. "But what's the use of dissecting any more, what possible use?" His hat was in his hand and he was heading for the door. "It's all simply maddening, and I'm a fool, a visionary fool, who can't change myself or alter events; powerless—" He halted, turned half about. Instinctive courtesy sprang to his lips. "Pardon me, Harry, for bothering you with all this when you can do nothing. I had no idea when I came of staying so long or—or of making a spectacle of myself." He smiled, almost his old smile. "Forgive me this time and

85

I promise never to do it again, never." He turned once more to the door. "Don't get up, old man. I can find my way out. Good-night."

"Steve! Wait!" Randall too was on his feet, a sudden premonition of things to come in his mind, a feeling, more than of pity, for the intention he read clear in the other's face. "Don't go yet—don't go at all. Stay with me to-night, please."

"Stay!" Armstrong too understood, and, understanding, smiled; a smile the other man never forgot. "Stay—to-night?... No, thank you. I appreciate your motive," hurriedly, "don't fancy it's not that; but—" no questioning that preventing gesture, no combating it—"but to-night I'm going to forget.... Yes, and to-morrow night, and the next—and the next!"

CHAPTER VIII

CATASTROPHE

Three evenings in succession a tall young man with an ulster turned up high above his chin and a derby hat lowered well over his eyes circled the block of which the Gleason lot and cottage was a part. The first time, in front of the house itself, he had merely halted, hands deep in his pockets, obviously uncertain; then, as though under strain of an immediate engagement beyond, had hastened on. The second time he had passed up the walk, half way to the door; had of a sudden changed his mind, and disappeared rapidly as before. The third evening, the present, however, there had been no uncertainty, no hesitation. Instead, he had walked straight to the knocker, and, a gray-haired man in lounging-jacket and carpet slippers answering his ring, had come to anchor in the familiar den. From his moorings in the single comfortable chair the place afforded, which had been compellingly pressed upon him, he was listening to the other's explanation.

"I think she'll return soon, though, very soon." Mr. Gleason adjusted his horn-rimmed eyeglasses and peered near-sightedly at his big open-faced silver watch. "She said she'd be back early and it's nearly nine now."

"Something going on, something important, I mean?"

"No; I don't think so. Just out for a little air, and dropped in on one of the girls maybe. She's got three freshmen she's coaching now, and with that out-of-town class and the house here—" The long bony fingers tapped absently tip to tip. "It's the only time that she has and I encourage, insist almost, that she go."

"Yes."

The tapping fingers went still.

"I think sometimes I'm a bit guilty that she at her age—that it should seem to be necessary, I mean—Maybe I imagine it, but it seems to me as though Elice was sort of fagged and different this winter."

The visitor unbuttoned his coat leisurely.

"I hadn't noticed it," he refuted.

"No? I'm glad to hear you say it. You'd have noticed, I guess, if any one. Probably it's all my imagination."

"Elice herself hasn't said anything, intimated anything?"

"Not a word or a hint. Certainly not." Something akin to surprise spoke in the quick reply. "She even wanted to take on another out-of-town class, but I vetoed that. She's as her mother was, Elice: always planning on doing just a little more."

"Than she ought, you think?"

"Yes."

Without apparent excuse, unconsciously, the visitor rebuttoned his double-breasted coat.

"Some people," he commented, "work—more than they ought to, to forget; and others again do—various things."

"What? I beg your pardon."

"To forget, to attain callousness, to cease to feel. There are many formulas tried, many."

"I fear I fail to understand."

"Doubtless. I don't understand myself. I was simply rambling. Pardon me."

Over the horn nose-glasses Mr. Gleason scrutinized the face of the younger man intently.

"Certainly. For what, though, I admit I'm mystified." He glanced away perfunctorily. "Everything is running normally, I suppose, in your department?"

"Yes, about as usual, I guess, practically so."

"Better than usual according to Dean Sanford," cheerfully. "He's inclined to brag a little this year, justifiedly, too, one must admit from the attendance."

"Yes, the attendance is excellent—among the students. Among the faculty—did the dean seem inclined to brag any on the faculty?"

"No; he only talked a few moments." Mr. Gleason produced the big timepiece again hastily. "Nine o'clock. I wonder what can be keeping Elice," he fidgeted.

The visitor smiled, an odd smile, neither of bitterness nor yet of amusement.

"Not inclined particularly to brag on his faculty, the dean, I gather?" returned Armstrong.

The older man straightened. Out of kindness he would retreat so far; but if pursued—

"No, he barely mentioned the faculty, as I remember."

"Not even the professor of chemistry?"

The horn-rimmed glasses had left their owner's nose and, as they had a way of doing when the old man was abstracted, swung like a pendulum from his fingers.

"Not even the professor of chemistry?" repeated Armstrong.

Very quietly the older man held his ground, very steadily.

"Just what is it you wish to know, Steve?" he asked directly. "You gathered, of course, it was a board meeting I referred to—and confidential naturally. I think I need say no more."

"No, no more, certainly. I was merely curious to know if you knew. You've satisfied my curiosity, I believe."

"Satisfied! I'm afraid you're taking a bit for granted. I repeat, if you'll tell me explicitly what you wish—"

"I was mistaken, then, after all," with a peculiar direct look. "You don't really know, Sanford didn't announce—I'm surprised. I never fancied he'd miss the opportunity. It's superhuman repression!"

For fully half a minute Mr. Gleason said nothing; then at the interrupting sound of footsteps in the storm vestibule, followed an instant later by the click of a latch-key, he leaned suddenly toward the younger man.

"That's Elice now," he said. The voice was almost childishly hurried and curious. "What was it that you wondered I didn't know, that Sanford didn't announce?"

From under shaded lids Armstrong observed the change and smiled. The smile vanished as a shadow passed through the entrance.

"I merely marvelled that the dean didn't announce that there would be no professor of chemistry after another week, the close of the present semester," he said evenly. "That is, until a new one is appointed."

"Steve!" The old man's face went gray,—gray as the face of a believer whose gods have been offered sacrilege. In the silence the shadow advanced to the doorway of the room itself; very real, paused there waiting, all-seeing, listening. "You mean you're leaving the department then, quitting for good?"

"For good, no, hardly." Again a laugh, but tense now, forced. "Nor quitting. In plain English I mean I'm kicked out, fired. By request, very insistent request, I've resigned." With an effort he met the girl's eyes fairly. "I've babbled my last lecture in college halls, piped my swan song. The curtain is down, the orchestra has packed its instruments. Only the echo now remains."

"Tell me about it, Steve." The old man had gone, dodderingly, on a pitifully transparent pretext. The girl had tossed coat and gloves on one chair and herself had taken another, removing her hat as she spoke.

"Begin at the beginning and tell me what's the matter—what this all means."

"There is no beginning that I know of," with a shrug that fell far short of the indifferent. "What it means I've already told you."

The hat followed the coat, hanging where it caught on the latter by one pin. "Let's not dissimulate for the present," pleaded the girl, "or juggle words. There's a time for everything."

"And the present?"

"Don't, please! As a favor, if you wish. Begin at the beginning."

"I repeat, there is none to my knowledge. There's only an end."

"The end, then," swiftly; "the reason for it. Don't you wish to tell me?"

"No, I don't wish to. I intend to tell you, however. It was all regular, my retirement; no one at fault among the powers that are. I had been warned—and failed to profit. It was very regular."

"Yes, yes; but the reason! Tell me that."

"Certainly. I was just coming to it. I failed to materialize at the department two days in succession. I overslept."

"Steve Armstrong! Steve—what do you fancy I'm made of! Do you mean to tell me or merely to—dissect?"

"No, not dissect, to tell you. That's why I came; to tell you several things, this among the rest. Elice, don't do that, don't cry. Please!—I don't intend to be a brute, I didn't mean anything. I'm simply ashamed to tell you straight from the shoulder. I'm down in the gutter. You'll hear, though, anyway. I might better—I was drunk, irresponsible, two days in succession. That's all."

"You—that way; you, Steve Armstrong!" No tears now, no hysterics; just steady, unbelieving expectancy. "I can't believe it—won't. You're playing with me."

"No, it's true. I won't say 'God knows it's true.' I'm not dog enough yet to—blaspheme. It's simply true."

"Steve!" The girl was on her feet, half way to him. "I never dreamed, never—You poor boy!"

"Elice, don't—don't touch me. I ask it—don't!"

"What—you can't mean—that!"

"Yes. Sit down, please." The voice was thick. "I have several things to tell you. This was only one."

For long, interminably long it seemed to the watcher, the girl stood where she had paused, midway; the figure of her still, too still, her face shading first red to the ear tips, then slowly colorless as understanding drove home. A half-minute probably, in reality, immeasurably longer to them both it seemed, she stood so. Without a word she went back to her seat, remained there, unnaturally still, her arms, bare to the elbow in half sleeves, forming a great white V as the clasped hands lay motionless in her lap.

For another half-minute no word was spoken, no sound from without drifted into the room. Suddenly the girl turned, her great dark eyes met those of the man, held them steadily.

"You said there was something else you wished to tell me. I can't imagine anything more, anything you didn't tell just now. However, I'm listening."

The man said nothing, nor moved—just looked at her.

"I repeat, I'm listening."

"Yes, I notice." Armstrong pulled himself together absently. "I was thinking of something else; I'd forgotten momentarily. I always was an absent-minded specimen; and lately—I've been worse than usual lately."

The girl merely waited this time, the great brown eyes wide and dry.

"When it comes to telling you, though," stumbled on the man, "what I came to tell you to-night, what I don't wish to tell you but must— Elice, don't look at me, please; don't! My nerve's gone. Don't you wish to ask me questions instead?"

"Perhaps," obediently the girl turned away, "after you've made things clear a bit. Don't fancy I'm trying to make it hard for you. I'm not, only, only—Remember, I'm all in the dark yet, all confused."

"Yes, I know—and I'm to blame. I've been trying for a week to bring myself to tell you, one thing at a time; but I couldn't, and now— everything's tumbled on my head together now."

"Everything? Steve, begin somewhere, anywhere. Don't suggest things; tell me. It's been ten days since you called last. Why was that?"

"I was afraid. I tried to come, but I couldn't."

"Afraid of what?"

"Of you, of myself, of life. I've known that long to a certainty that the play was over between you and me, but I couldn't bring myself to say the word. It's just this I was afraid of. This!"

"You mean to tell me now that all is over?" Unconsciously this time the girl had shifted facing; quietly—again, too quietly—was putting the query direct: "That's what you're telling me now?"

"Yes."

"And why—Am I the cause—have I by word or act—have I?"

"No."

"Is it because you've lost your chair in the University?"

"No."

"Why, then?"

"Because we've ceased to be necessary to each other, have grown apart."

"You think we've changed?... I've not changed."

"No. It's I who have changed, have grown away from you."

"Since when? Let's have it all. Let's understand everything. Since when?"

"I don't know when, can't set a date. I merely know."

"That—that you don't care for me any more?"

"Steve!" The girl was on her feet. "I never dreamed, never—You poor boy!"

A halt, a long, long halt.

"Yes, Elice," said a voice at last. "I've found out that I don't care for you any more."

As before, the girl said nothing, never stirred.

"I shan't try to defend myself, try to explain," stumbled on the man. "I couldn't if I would. The thing has simply come about—I wish to ask you to release me."

"Steve!" Of a sudden the girl was on her feet, the forced composure of a moment ago in tatters, the tiny hands locked tight. "I can't believe it, can't credit it. I love you, Steve, in spite of all you've told me; more, because you need me more now." The locked fingers opened. She came a step forward in mute appeal. "Tell me that you don't mean it, that you're merely acting, that, that—" As suddenly she halted. Her face hidden in her hands, she dropped back into the seat. "Forget, please," she halted, "that I did that. I didn't mean to. I—I—forget it."

"Elice—dear!" Aroused beyond his purpose, his determination, the man sprang from his seat, his eyes ablaze, glorious. "Elice—"

"No, not pity! Never, a thousand times no! Leave me alone a minute. I release you, yes, yes; but don't come near me now. I'm hysterical and irresponsible. Don't, please!"

Precisely where he stood Armstrong paused, looking down. After that first involuntary sound he had not spoken or come closer. He merely remained there, waiting, looking; and as he did so, though the room was far from close, drops of sweat gathered on his forehead and beneath his eyes. With a restless hand he brushed them away and sat down. Another minute passed, two perhaps; then suddenly, interrupting, incongruous, there sounded the strained rasp of his laugh.

"Elice," followed a voice, "aren't you through—nearly?" Again the laugh; grating, unmirthful. "I've done this sort of thing identically in novels several times, done it realistically, I thought; but it never took this long by minutes. Aren't you almost through?"

Surprised out of herself the girl looked up, incredulous.

"Something must be wrong, art or reality, one or the other. I—I wonder—which was wrong, Elice?"

As suddenly as the mood of abandon had come it passed; incredulity, its successor, as well. In the space of seconds the miracle was wrought, and another woman absolutely sat there looking forth from the brown eyes of Elice Gleason.

"Steve! I thought I was ready for anything after what you just told me, what you just asked. But this deliberate—insult.... Did you mean it, Steve, really; or are you merely acting?... Don't look away; this means the world to you and me, and I want to be sure, now.... Did you mean it, Steve, the way you did it, deliberately? Tell me."

"Mean it? Certainly. It's important, what I asked, from an artist's point of view. Either I was wrong or else reality is—overdone.... Repression's the word, all critics agree, repression invariably."

"Steve Armstrong! Stop! I won't stand it. Listen. It's unbelievable, but I must take you at your word—your own word. Do you mean exactly what you've said, and done?"

Again the moisture sprang to Armstrong's face, but this time there was no attempt at procrastination.

"Yes, Elice," he said, and looked her fair.

"Yes? Think. This is final."

"Yes."

An instant the look held; the brown eyes dropped.

"I repeat, then, you are released, free." She sat very still. "Is there anything else you wish to say?"

"Perhaps. I don't know.... You mean, if I have I'm to say it now. I can't come again.... You're not going to forgive me?"

"Forgive? Certainly, if there is anything to forgive. I had no thought otherwise."

"I'm not to come again, though. You mean that?"

"I fail to see the object.... To use an expression of your own, it's desecration to disturb the corpse."

"Even if—"

"Let's not argue about nothing. I'm not cursed with nerves ordinarily, but there are times—" She arose slowly, stood there beside her chair, gracefully slender, gracefully imperious. "You've chosen deliberately, you know."

"Yes, I know." Armstrong too had arisen in his dismissal, involuntarily obedient. "But you said, before I told you, before you understood, that afterward, perhaps—You remember you said that?"

"Yes; I remember. Things are changed now, though. What I had in mind you've answered yourself.... One thing I would like to ask, however, one thing that I hope you will answer truly, no matter whether it hurts me or not. It's this: Was I to blame in any way whatever, by word or act or suggestion, for your losing your place in the University? Will you answer me that—and truly?"

From the chair where he had thrown it down Armstrong took up the long ulster and buttoned it mechanically to his throat.

"No, Elice," he repeated; "you're not at fault in any way, by word or act or suggestion. There's no one at fault except myself."

"Thank you. I would always have feared, if I hadn't asked, that somehow unintentionally—" She was silent.

Armstrong hesitated, waiting until there was no longer hope.

"You have nothing else you wish to say, then?" he asked at last.

"Nothing; unless it is this, that you know already: I shall always believe in you, Steve, always."

"Believe in me!" The shade of the old ironic smile did duty. "You think I shall still become wealthy and famous?"

"Perhaps not," swiftly. "I never demanded either qualification of you. Why should I lie now? Both are right and desirable in their place, provided they come normally; but their place is second, not first. You know what I mean. I believe that you will always be clean and fair and likeable—always."

Involuntarily the man turned away, until his face was hidden.

"You believe this, and still—you don't give advice or—or warning?"

"I repeat, I believe in you. Even if it weren't an insult advice would not be necessary."

A last second they stood there, so near, so very near together and still so infinitely far apart. Dully, almost ploddingly, the man turned to leave.

"Thank you, Elice," he said. "That's probably the last kind word I'll hear for a long time. Perhaps, too, it's justified, perhaps—who knows? Good-night and—good-bye."

The girl did not follow him, did not move.

"Good-bye, Steve," she echoed.

BOOK II

CHAPTER I

ANTICIPATION

"Are you given to remembering dates, Elice?"

There had been a pause,—one of the inevitable, normal pauses that occur when two people who are intimate are alone and conversation drifts where it will. Into this particular void, without preamble, entered this question.

"Sometimes. Why?"

"Not always, then?"

"No. I haven't any particular tendency that way that I know of. Possibly I'm not yet old enough for it to develop."

"To be more specific, then, to-day is December the sixth." Darley Roberts' eyelids narrowed whimsically. "Does that particular date have any special significance, recall anything out of the ordinary to you?"

Elice Gleason glanced up from the four-leafed clover she was bringing to life on the scrap of linen in her lap, and looked at her companion thoughtfully.

"From the way you come at me, point blank," she smiled, "I have no doubt it should. Your chance questions, I've discovered, always do have a string attached to them somewhere. But just at this particular moment I admit December the sixth recalls nothing in particular."

"Not even when I add, at approximately eight o'clock in the evening? It's that now. I've been consulting the timepiece over there."

"No; not even that. I'm more and more convinced it's a distinct lapse on my part; but again I'm compelled to confess incompetency. When did what happen at approximately eight P.M. on December the sixth?"

Darley Roberts stroked his great chin with reminiscent deliberation.

"On December sixth, at eight o'clock P.M., precisely one year ago," he explained minutely, "a certain man called on a certain young woman of his acquaintance for the first time. It was, I am reliably informed, a momentous occasion for him. Moreover he—Had you really forgotten, Elice?"

"Yes—the date."

"Strange. I hadn't. Perhaps, though, it meant more to me than to you." He laughed peculiarly. "I fancy I didn't tell you at the time that it was the first call I'd ever made on a young woman in my life." He laughed again with tolerant amusement. "I was thirty-three years old then, too."

The girl drew a thread of green from a bundle of silk in her lap deliberately. "No; you never told me that," she corroborated.

The wrinkles gathering about Darley Roberts' eyes suddenly deepened, infallible precursor of the unexpected.

"By the way," he digressed, "I'm growing curious to know what you do with those things you're embroidering, those—"

"Lunch cloths?"

"That's it, lunch cloths. The present makes seven, one after the other, you've completed. I've kept count."

"Curious, you say?" The girl laughed softly. "And still you've never asked."

"No. I fancied there'd ultimately be an end, a variation at least; but it seems I was mistaken. Do you expect to keep them, as a man does a case of razors, one for each day of the week?"

Again the soft little amused laugh.

"Hardly. I sell them. There are five more in prospect—an even dozen."

"Oh. I wondered."

Another void; an equally abrupt return.

"To come back to the date," recalled the man, "I remembered it distinctly this morning when I tore the top leaf off the desk-pad. It stood out as though it were printed in red ink, like the date of a holiday. I—do I show signs of becoming senile—childish, Elice?"

"Not that I've noticed. You seem normal."

"Nor irresponsible—moonstruck—nothing of that kind?"

"No."

"I'm glad to hear it. I didn't know.... Somehow this morning the sight of that date made me do a thing I haven't done since—I don't know when. I had a consuming desire to celebrate."

The girl's head was bent low, the better to see her work.

"Yes?" she said.

Again the man stroked his chin, with the former movement of whimsical deliberation.

"Do you know what people down town, people I do business with, call me, Elice?" he asked.

"No."

"Never heard of 'old man' Roberts?"

"No," again.

"Well, that's me—old man Roberts—old man—thirty-four.... By the way, what do you call me, Elice?"

"Mr. Roberts," steadily.

"Not Darley; not once in all this last year?"

No answer.

"Not Darley—even once?"

"I think not."

The eyes of the man smiled, the eyes only.

"To return again, old man Roberts had a desire to celebrate. The date was on his brain. He didn't even take off his coat after he'd seen it—normally the old man works in his shirt-sleeves, you know—he just walked back from his private room into the general office. 'To-day's a holiday,' he said.

"They stared, the office force—there are seven of them. They didn't say a word; they just stared.

"'I say to-day's a holiday,' the old man repeated, 'shut up shop.'"

There was a silence. In it Miss Gleason glanced up—into two eyes smiling out of a blank face. Her own dropped. Simultaneously, also, her ears tinged scarlet.

Darley Roberts laughed a low tolerant laugh at his own expense.

"Still think I wasn't irresponsible—moonstruck—nothing of the kind?"

"No—Mr. Roberts."

"Wait. After the force had gone, still staring, the old man went back to his desk. He looked up a number in the telephone directory. 'Mr. Herbert? Roberts, Darley Roberts.—I'd like to see you personally. Yes, at once. I'm waiting.'"

Again the girl glanced up; something made her. And again she encountered those same eyes smiling out of a masked face.

"The old man waited; ten minutes maybe. He didn't do a thing; just waited. Then events came to pass." Once more the little throaty laugh. "'Mr. Herbert,' he said, 'your house you advertise for sale. How much this morning?'

"Mr. Herbert seemed surprised, distinctly surprised. He was only half through the door at the time.

"'Eighteen thousand dollars. It cost twenty,'—after he's caught his breath.

"'It cost *you* fifteen even. I've been to some trouble to find out.'

"'You can't know the place, Mr.—Mr. Roberts.'

"'Yes. Top of the hill. Faces east and north. Terra cotta, brick. For reasons you know best it's been vacant for a month now.'

"'You can't know the inside, I mean. It's finished in solid hardwood, every inch.'

"'Yes, I've seen it; oak in front, mahogany in the dining-room, rosewood in the den. I've seen it.'

"'When? I've lived there nine years until just lately. Not in that time.'

"'Yes, during that time. I was at a party there once,—a university party which Mrs. Herbert gave.'

"'All right. Maybe you know.'

"'Unquestionably. I repeat the place cost you fifteen thousand.'

"'The price now is eighteen.'

"'You don't wish to sell—at fifteen?'

"'No.'

"'That's all, then.'

"'Roberts—confound it—'

"'I'm sorry to have bothered you. I thought you wished to sell.'

"'I've got to, but I don't have to give it away.'

"'I repeat I'm sorry to have bothered you.'

"'I'll see you again; to-morrow perhaps—'

"'I shall be very busy to-morrow. To-day's a holiday.'

"'A holiday! Anyway I haven't the abstract.'

"'Unnecessary. I said I knew all about the place. I see the deed there in your pocket. You anticipated, I see.'

"'Well, of all the inexplicable hurry!'

"'Shall I write you a check for—fifteen thousand?'"

Darley Roberts halted. For the third time he laughed.

"You gather, perhaps," he said, "that I bought a house this morning. Afterward I bought a few other things—just a few. After that I moved in; into two rooms. I've had rather a busy day, all told, celebrating—celebrating December the sixth.... How about it, Elice, now that I've elaborated. Any signs of senility, irresponsibility, yet?"

"No," very steadily. "It seems perfectly natural to me for a man to want a house."

"Perhaps you're right. Yes; I do want a house, no doubt about it; particularly that house. I've been intending to own it sometime for quite a spell—for some eight years now; to be exact, since the time I saw it before.... You know the place, don't you?"

"Yes, very well."

"I fancied so.... By the way, do you recall that—occasion I referred to?"

"Indistinctly."

"I fancied that too.... You don't remember by any chance what a lion I was that night?"

"No, Mr. Roberts."

"Not 'no, Darley'?"

"No."

"Not even yet; and it's been a year!... As I was about to say, though, I recall distinctly. I remember I had a perfectly delightful time — listening to the others' conversation. Likewise dancing — with myself in a shadowy corner. Also eating lunch — with myself later. I had ample time to think — and I decided eventually that there'd been a slight mistake somehow when my name got on the list.... I liked the house, though, very much; so much that I decided to buy it sometime — at a nominal figure. I didn't feel peculiarly generous that night when I made the decision.... Last of all, I recall I met a girl; rather young then, but rather pleasant also, I thought. She talked to me for an entire minute. I know because I held my breath the while, and that's my limit. She was the only one who apparently did see me that night, though. Perhaps her being rather young was why."

The voice ceased. The speaker looked at the listener. Simultaneously the listener looked at the speaker. They smiled, companionably, understandingly.

"That's all, I believe, I have to impart concerning December the sixth, all concerning the celebration. That is —" of a sudden the bantering voice was serious and low — "that is, unless there's something more you'd like to know."

The girl was busy with the clover again, very busy.

"I think you've told me all there is to tell," she said steadily. "I understand."

Darley Roberts waited; but that was all.

"Very well." The voice was normal again, tolerant, non-committal. "It's your turn, then. I fear I'm becoming positively loquacious. I monopolize the conversation. Let's hear your report since — Thanksgiving, I believe, — the last time I heard it."

For some reason the girl lost interest in her work. At least there seemed less need of immediate haste. She rolled the silks and the linen together with a little unconscious sigh of relief.

"Since Thanksgiving," she said, "I've cooked eighteen meals for father and myself. I've been out of town once, coached two thick heads twice each, attended one bridge party—or was it five hundred? I believe that's all."

"Not had a call from Miss Simpson?" smilingly.

"How did you know?"

"I don't know. I asked you."

"Yes; Agnes called—of course."

"What report of your friends the Randalls, then?"

"Shame on you—really."

"No. I didn't mean it that way—really. You know it. I'm interested because you are. How are things coming on with them?"

The girl fingered the roll in her lap absently. "Badly, I'm afraid. Margery's gone to Chicago to visit her cousin, and shop. She can't seem to realize—or won't. I went over and baked some things for Harry yesterday. He's dismissed the maid they had and the place looks as cheerful as a barn. I didn't even see him."

"You noticed the house, though, doubtless. Much new furniture about?"

"Yes, for the dining-room; a complete new suite, sideboard and all, in weathered oak. It's dear.... How in the world did you know, though?"

"A big rug, too, and curtains, and—a lot of things?"

"How did you know, you? Tell me that."

"Would you say it was worth four hundred dollars in all, what you saw?" The eyes were smiling again.

"Perhaps. I don't know. I have never bought such things.... You haven't answered my question yet."

"I know because Mr. Randall told me. He also requested me, as a favor, to ask you about them instead of going to the house myself."

"Which means you made him a loan to pay the bill. Are you a friend of Harry's?"

"A loan, yes. A friend—only as your friends are mine."

"It's too bad, a burning shame—when Harry works so hard, too." The girl winked fast, against her will. "I can't quite forgive Margery."

"For going to Chicago?"

"For everything. For that too."

"Not if I told you I advised her to go?"

"You!" In astonishment complete the girl stared. "You advised her to go?"

"Yes, the same day I made Randall the loan. It was really a coincidence. I wondered they didn't meet in the elevator."

"A lawyer in a little town like this, with several departments in his business, comes in contact with a variety of things," he commented after a moment.

"Tell me about Margery." The girl seemed to have heard that suggestion only. "I can't understand, can't believe—really."

For a moment Roberts was silent. There was no banter in his manner when he looked up at last.

"I didn't tell you this merely to gossip," he said slowly; "I think you appreciate that without my saying it; but somehow I felt that you ought to know—that if any one could do any good there it is you. I never met either of them before, that's another coincidence; but from what you've told me and the little I saw of them both that day, I felt dead sorry. Besides, life's so short, and I hate—divorce."

"You can't mean it has come to that?"

"It hadn't come, but it was coming fast. She visited me first. From there she was going straight to her father—to stay."

"It's horrible, simply horrible—and so unjustified! You induced her, though, to go to Chicago instead?"

"It was a compromise, a play for time. I tried to get her to go back home, but she refused, positively. The only alternative seemed to be to get her away—quick.... Was I right?"

"Yes, I think so, under the circumstances. But the trouble itself, I can't understand yet—Was it that abominable furniture?"

"Partly. At least that was the final straw, the match to the fuse. The whole thing had been gathering slowly for a long time. I didn't get the entire story, of course. She wasn't exactly coherent. It seems she ordered it on her own responsibility, and when the goods were delivered—the thing was merely inevitable, some time—that was all."

"Inevitable? No. It was abominable of Margery—unforgivable."

"I don't know about that; in fact I'm inclined to differ. I still maintain it was inevitable."

"Inevitable fiddlesticks! Harry is the best-natured man alive, and generous. He's been too generous, too easy; that's the trouble."

"'Generous?'" gently. "'Generous?'... Is it generous for a man with nothing and no prospect of anything to take a girl out of a home where money was never a consideration, and transplant her into another where practically it is the only thought?... 'Generous' for his own pleasure, to undertake to teach her a financial lesson he knew to a moral certainty in advance she could never learn? Do you honestly call that 'generous'?"

"But she could learn. It—was her duty."

"Duty!" Roberts laughed tolerantly. "Is 'duty' in the dictionary you use a synonym for 'cooking' and 'scrubbing' and 'drudgery'? Is that your interpretation?"

"Sometimes—in this case, yes; for a time."

"Permanently, you mean?"

"No; for a time—until Harry got on his feet."

"He'll never get on his feet unaided. Instead he'll get more and more wobbly all the time. The past proves the future. He's proved it."

"You're simply horrid." There were real tears in the girl's eyes now, not a mere premonition. "I'm sorry I ever told you anything about them."

"I know I'm horrid, grant it. A friend I once had told me I was a fish,—cold-blooded like one. Nature made me that way, you see, so I can't help it. And still I'm inclined to believe if Mrs. Randall had chanced to select any other lawyer in town there'd be a real separation, instead of one in prospect, right now."

Elice Gleason looked up penitently.

"I'm sorry," she said simply. "I didn't mean that."

"I don't doubt it," equally simply.

"You're so blunt and logical though; so—abstract."

"Yes; I am that way."

The girl drew a long breath. Seemingly, after all, the victory was hers.

"Well, what are we going to do about it? We, their friends, have to do something."

"Yes, that's the question—what?"

"Margery will never go back now of herself. I know her."

"No; she'll never go back of herself, never. Do you blame her?"

No answer. The query was sudden.

"Honest, do you blame her?" insistently.

"I thought I did. I don't know—I don't know."

"Does 'love, honor, and obey' mean 'wash, bake, and scrub' to a girl who has never in her life before done any of the three?"

Still silence.

"Would you, if you were in her place, come back—would you?"

"I?" It was almost a gasp. "I'm not like Margery. I've counted pennies all my life." A sudden flame. "But why do you bring me in?"

"Why? That's true. I had no right. I apologize. To come back to Mrs. Randall. Do you still blame her?"

"No, I don't believe I do. I ought to, I feel that; but I don't. It's tangled, tangled!"

"Yes. It's the first symptom of divorce."

The girl flashed him a sudden look.

"And you hate divorce. You just said so."

"From the bottom of my soul. I meant it."

Miss Gleason flashed a second look. Suddenly, unaccountably, she held the reins.

"What's to be done then? Margery is as she is, we both know that; and—and Harry loves her, we both know that, too. What do you suggest?"

"I?" Roberts smiled, his slow smile. "I'm her lawyer and—abstract. Besides, her father is wealthy. There'd be a fat fee if she returned to him."

"You forget that I apologized."

"That's right. I'm always forgetting." Apparently he did not remember even yet.

"You've neglected to answer my question," impatiently. "I repeat: what are you going to do about it?"

"I asked your solution first. Do you give it up?"

"Yes," with a little gesture; "I give it up."

Darley Roberts smiled; a contagious, convincing smile.

"Very well, I'll try then," he said. "I shan't promise anything. I'll simply try."

"Try how?"

Again Roberts smiled; but through whimsically narrowed lids now.

"I'm not sure of the details yet myself. I merely have an idea. There's an old adage concerning Mahomet and the mountain, you know."

"And in this case Margery represents the mountain?"

"Yes."

Unconsciously the girl's color heightened.

"You really fancy," swiftly, "that Harry can be stirred up enough, can be made practical enough—you forget you said a moment ago that he would never advance financially."

"No. The adage will have to be adjusted a bit to meet the requirements. He'll have to be carried there."

Elice Gleason drew a quick little breath of understanding and something more.

"If you'll do this for one almost a stranger, one wonders what you would do for a friend," she said; "one—wonders."

For an instant the man said nothing; abruptly, dismissing the subject, he arose.

"There's just one other thing that I meant to tell you," he said; "something that perhaps you know already. I'm pretty busy and I don't always find time to read the local news. So it's not unusual that I didn't know before. Steve Armstrong is back."

Quietly the girl arose also, stood so very still.

"Yes," she said. "He's been back a week. He's working in the big drug-store on the corner, Shaw's place, in the laboratory."

"That's all, then. I thought perhaps you didn't know."

For an instant the girl was silent; she looked her companion full in the face.

"He called the afternoon he came. He was almost—pitiable. Father came home finally."

"Elice!"

Their eyes held. Not three feet separate they stood there; but neither stirred.

"Mr. Roberts."

In silence the man put on top-coat and gloves; not hastily, nor yet lingeringly. Equally naturally he picked up his hat.

"December the sixth," he said. "One whole year. To-morrow will be the seventh—and business—battle, again." For the first time he dallied, the big soft felt hat turning absently in his hand. "Somehow I'd hoped a lot for the sixth, planned a lot—and now it's past." His eyes shifted, fastened elsewhere compellingly.

"It is all past, all over, gone into history, isn't it, Elice?"

"Yes, it's past, Mr. Roberts."

"Not even 'past, Darley,' not even that—yet?"

The brown eyes dropped. They had fought their fight and won—for December the sixth.

"No. Not even that—yet," she said.

CHAPTER II

ACQUAINTANCE

At the corner next beyond the Gleason home Darley Roberts caught the nine o'clock car, and remained on it until the end of the division, practically the extreme opposite edge of the town, was reached. He was the last passenger to leave, and as the motorman was reversing the trolley he paused a moment in the vestibule.

"Normal load was it, Johnson?" he asked the conductor. "You rang up twenty-four fares, I noticed."

The man looked consciously surprised to be called by name.

"Yes, Mr. Roberts," he said; "we carry anywhere between twenty and thirty at this time of night."

"How about the next trip, nine-thirty?"

"Better yet if anything."

"And the next, the last?"

"Best of all. The straps are nearly always loaded."

Roberts buttoned up his coat deliberately.

"Think it would pay to run a couple of hours longer?" he asked, and this time the conductor all but flushed at the unexpected confidence.

"Yes; I'm sure it would, Mr. Roberts; especially when the school's in session. The boys would ride half the night if they could."

"There seems to be a good deal in that. By the way, you have only one shift on this car now, I understand."

It was the long-hoped-for opportunity and Johnson grew eloquent.

"Right you are, and it's the dog's life for us men. I've had only one hot meal a day since I took the job." He searched the impassive face before him with a glance. "If the schedule was stretched a little, now, at either end and a second shift added —"

"That's a good idea. I'm glad it occurred to you. Better speak to the superintendent about it yourself; he'll see the point." Roberts alighted deliberately. "Any suggestion you men in the service make is valuable." As he vanished up the street toward his destination, in the fulness of knowledge that the contemplated suggestion had been decided from the turning of the first wheel on the system, he left behind him a man imbued with an *esprit de corps* that was to grow and leaven the entire working force. It took but a minute all told!

Five minutes later, in the half dark doorway of a cottage on a side street, he was face to face with Harry Randall.

"Pardon me if I intrude," he was saying, "but I'm going out of town to-morrow and I wish to talk with you a bit before I go. Can you spare me a little time?"

"Certainly." Randall's manner was decidedly stiff. Nevertheless he led the way through the vestibule and living-room to the dining-room beyond. There he halted significantly. "By the way," he began, "the furniture I mentioned —"

"Damn the furniture!" Roberts met his host's look steadily. "You know me better than that, by reputation if nothing more. I said I wished to talk with you. May I?"

Randall colored, and the stiffness vanished as by a miracle.

"Pardon me," he said. "I've got a sort of den upstairs where I do my work." Again he led the way. "My wife's out of town, though, now, and things are a bit mussy."

Roberts made no comment, and they mounted the stairs in silence.

Inside the room the visitor swept the place with a single all-including glance. Thereafter, apparently, he observed nothing.

"First of all, then," he initiated bluntly, "do I intrude? If so, I can tell my business in five minutes; if not, we might possibly become acquainted."

Again Randall colored; then he smiled, his saving quality.

"Not in the least. It's Friday night, you know. In addition I was a bit lonely. I'm distinctly glad to see you."

"Which, interpreted, means glad to see any one."

"Yes, I suppose so."

For an instant the old odd smile shone in Roberts' eyes, then it disappeared, leaving them normal, inscrutable.

"To begin with, then, I came primarily to talk about Steve Armstrong. I believe he's a friend of yours."

"Yes." A halt, then the query direct returned. "Is he of yours?"

"I'll answer that question later, if you please. At least he's the one adult to date I can remember who ever called me by my first name. Did you know that he'd returned to town?"

"Yes. He was here last night."

"Responsible, was he?"

"Mr. Roberts!" Randall flushed like a woman with strangers. "Pardon me, but there are some questions I can't answer—at least until you answer my own of a moment ago."

"I understand perfectly. Also, contrary to your suspicion, I didn't avoid your question to make it difficult for you. It requires two to be friends. Enmities I, personally, have none. Life's too short and too busy. If it will assist you any, I met Armstrong in the street this evening face to face, and he declined to speak. I judge he's no friend to me. Am I any more clear?"

"Yes," simply.

"Do you wish to answer my question now, then?"

"I judge you have a good reason for asking. He was not responsible, wholly."

"Not even decently so?"

"Hardly."

"I gathered as much from his appearance to-night. It was the first time I'd seen him in nearly a year. You know the whole story between Armstrong and myself, I take it?"

"Yes," once more.

"And your sympathy is naturally with him."

"It has been."

"And now—"

The smile that made Randall's face boyish came into being.

"I'm deferring judgment now—and observing."

"I fear I can't help you much there," said Darley, shortly. "I wished to discuss the future a bit, not the past. The last time I talked with Armstrong he was impossible. I think you know what I mean. All men are that way when they lose their nerve and drown the corpse. What I wish to ask of you is whether the thing was justified. I'm not artistic. I don't brag of it—I admit it. You're different; your opinion is of value. Commercially, he's an impossibility. He couldn't hold a place if he had it—any place. I don't need to tell you that either. As a writer—can he write, or can't he?"

Harry Randall took off his big eyeglasses and polished one lens and then the other.

"In my opinion, yes—and no." He held the glasses to the light, seemed satisfied, and placed them carefully on his nose. "A great writer—he'll never be that. It takes nerve and infinite patience to be anything great, and Steve invariably loses his nerve too soon. He lacks just that much of being big. As for ability, the spark—he's got it, Roberts, as certainly as you and I are sitting here. Elementally, he's a child and will always remain a child. I think most artists are more or less so. Children can't bear criticism or delay—uncertain delay— that's Steve. On the other hand, if he were encouraged, kept free on the financial side, left at liberty to work when he felt the mood, and then only, then—I realize it's a big 'if' and a big contract for some one—he'd make good. Have I answered your question?"

"Yes. And here's another: Is it worth while?"

"To bolster him, you mean; to 'pull him out of the mud,' to use his own phrase?"

"No; that would be a waste of energy. I mean to keep him out permanently, to continue pulling indefinitely."

For a long time the two men sat in silence.

"God knows," said Randall at last. "I've asked myself the same question for years—and couldn't answer it. It's as big as the universe. Steve is simply an atom. It's unanswerable."

In the pause following Roberts lit one of the seemingly inexhaustible black cigars, after proffering its mate. Again the two sat there, the blue haze of mutual understanding gathering between them.

"I say it's unanswerable," repeated Randall. "It's the old problem of the young supporting the uselessly old, the well serving the incurably diseased. It means eternal vigilance from some one, eternal sacrifice. It's insoluble, neither more nor less."

"Yes," said Roberts. "I've found it so—insoluble. Particularly so in this case."

Slowly Randall's glance lifted, met the other's eyes. That instant, as a flame is born, came full understanding between them.

"Yes, particularly so in this case," echoed Roberts; "for it means a woman's sacrifice, one particular woman's sacrifice. Nothing else in the world will do—nothing."

It was the beginning of personal confidence, the halting-point for conversation between these two. Both knew it and neither crossed the line. They merely waited until a digression should come naturally. Roberts it was who at last introduced it, and in a manner so matter of fact that the other was all but deceived.

"Has Armstrong been doing anything lately in a literary way—anything, I mean, that justifies your opinion?" he asked abruptly.

"No, not that I know of; absolutely nothing."

"You're relying, then, on past impressions merely."

"Yes; specifically the last novel he wrote,—the one of a year or a year and a half or so ago."

"You haven't by any chance a copy of the manuscript, I suppose?"

"No."

"You could doubtless get it, however?"

"I think so—unless some time he became morbid and burned it."

"He hasn't done that; I know him. He might threaten; but to do it—he'd as probably go hungry. Get it some time, will you?"

"I will if you request. You don't wish it for yourself, do you?"

"No, not for myself. Perhaps not at all. I've not decided yet. Anyway get it, please, and be ready if I should ask." He flashed a look no man had ever questioned, could question. "You don't doubt my motive?"

"No. The manuscript will be ready. I'll answer for that."

No further question of interest was asked, no additional hint of purpose proffered. The subject merely dropped, as in the beginning it had merely begun. In some ways they were similar, these two men in general so dissimilar.

"I had another object in calling to-night," said Roberts, and again the announcement was made without preface. "The opportunity to buy a house presented itself to-day and I accepted. Perhaps you know the place,—J. C. Herbert's, on top of the hill."

"Yes." Open wonder spoke in the voice, open mystification. "Yes, I know it."

"It's been vacant for some time. I moved this afternoon, just into a couple of rooms. My boy is there now trying to warm up the place; but even then it won't be particularly inviting. Besides, I'm out of town quite a bit and in the future am likely to be called away still more. It occurred to me that if I could find some married people whom I trusted, who would take a personal interest in it and make it a home, it would be pleasanter for me than being tucked away in a couple of rooms alone and the rest of the barn empty."

"Yes," repeated Randall, impersonally, "I think I appreciate your point of view. It's a little cheerless to be in a house alone."

"I wouldn't expect to interfere with them in any way," Roberts drifted on, "or live with them—nothing of the kind. As I said, I probably shouldn't even be there much; only at night. I'd expect to keep it up—coal and light and that sort of thing—just the same as I would have to do if I were alone. I'd naturally wish to help furnish it, too; the things that would inevitably fit in with it and wouldn't fit any place else. But the main thing would be to have somebody about to make my own corner livable, to sort of humanize the place. You catch my idea?"

"Yes, I think so." Harry Randall's hand was on his bald spot, caressing it absently. "Yes, I think so," he repeated.

"It's a big place, even larger than I remembered, when I went through it to-day," went on Roberts again. "It'll take considerable help to keep it up and some one will have to be about constantly to direct. I have the help in mind right now, competent too—I meet a lot of people in various ways and I've had the thing on my mind; but the supervision—it's simply out of the question with me at the present." He faced the other, looked at him straight. "Would you and Mrs. Randall care to accept the place as a home in return for taking the responsibility of up-keep from me?"

In the pause following Harry Randall's face went slowly red. Equally directly he met the other's look.

"Pardon me, Mr. Roberts," he said, "but Mrs. Randall and myself are not exactly objects of charity yet."

Darley Roberts' expression did not alter by so much as the twitching of a muscle.

"That was unjustified, Mr. Randall," he said evenly, "and you know it. Let me explain a bit further. I happen to have a house, but no home. By the same chance you are able to produce the reverse. Just why should it be an offence upon my part to suggest bringing the two together—for the mutual benefit of us both?"

"Why? Because it's unequal, it's patronage; and though I work for twelve hundred dollars a year, I'm still American born."

"Granted—the latter remark. I'm also American born, in the remotest corner of the most God-forsaken county in—I won't name the State; I might hurt some one's feelings." Roberts' big fingers were twitching in a way they had when something he had decided to do met with opposition. "Nevertheless I hope that fact doesn't make me wholly unreasonable. When it comes to patronage, we're all patronized: you do a kindness for a friend, without remuneration, and he accepts it; that's patronage. The University gives you a position as professor, out of a dozen applicants who could do equally well, and you accept gladly. That's favoritism, another word for patronage. A client comes to me and pays a fee for doing a certain labor, when my competitor across the street would perform it equally capably, and for perhaps a smaller fee. That's patronage. You patronize your tailor when you order a suit of clothes, the butcher when you buy a beefsteak. It's the basis of life, elemental. The very air you breathe is patronage. It costs you nothing, and you give nothing adequate in return. To characterize patronage as un-American, stultifying, is preposterous. Even if it were true in this case, you'd have to give another reason for offence. I refuse to consider it."

"Well, unbusinesslike then, if that is better."

"Unbusinesslike? Wait. In company with three other men I'm developing a silver mine down in Arizona. The mining claim belongs to a fifth man, belongs to him absolutely. He knows the metal is there as well as we do; but it's down under the ground, locked up tight in a million tons of rock. As it is now, so far as he's concerned, it might as well be on Mars. If left to himself alone he'd live and die and it would still be there. He hasn't the ability nor the means to make it of use. The other three men and myself have. We can develop it, and will; to our own purposes, share and share alike. According to your notion there's patronage somewhere; but exactly where? Point me the offence?"

Again Harry Randall caressed his bald crown. The argument was convincing, almost.

"The cases are not parallel," he combated weakly, "not even similar."

"And why not?" shortly. "I'm no longer a young man particularly. I've never had a place that I could call home in my life; never for a day that I can remember. I want one now, fancy I see the possibility of making one; a place where I can keep a friend now and then if I wish, where I could even order in a supper and entertain if I saw fit. I chance to have the ability to pay for the privilege, and am willing to pay. That's my affair. You chance to be able to make that home possible—and incidentally enjoy it yourself. It's like the silver mine,—mutual benefit, share and share alike. The cases seem to me parallel, quite parallel."

Opposite Harry Randall sat very still. In absent forgetfulness he polished the big glasses the second time and sprung them back carefully on his nose. But even yet he did not answer, merely sat there waiting; awaiting the moment to counter, to refute.

"Am I not right?" asked Roberts, bluntly. "Isn't the proposition logical?"

"Logical, yes. The logic is very good." Randall glanced up keenly. The moment for which he had been waiting had come, more quickly than he had expected. "So *good* in fact that I see but one fault."

"And that?"

This time the keen eyes smiled, very candidly.

"The sole fault, so far as I can see, is that you don't believe in it yourself."

For the space wherein one could count ten slowly the two men looked at each other; slowly, in turn, on Roberts' firm fighter's face there formed a smile, a peculiar, appreciative smile.

"Granted," he said. "I admit failure." The smile passed like a dropped curtain. "Moreover be assured I shall not dissimulate again. As a friend, or whatever you wish, however, I advise you to think carefully before you refuse an offer made in good faith and to your own advantage."

Listening, Harry Randall straightened. His lips closed tightly for a second. "You mean, I presume," the words were painfully exact, "to remind me that you hold my note for four hundred dollars, and to imply—" he halted significantly.

For a moment the other man said nothing, the face of him told nothing. Then deliberately, from an inner pocket, he drew out a leather wallet, from the wallet a strip of paper, and held it so the other could read. Still without a word he tore it to bits.

"The devil take your note!" he observed, succinctly and without heat.

"Mr. Roberts, you—" Randall's face was crimson, "you—"

"Yes—I—"

"You didn't mean—that, then, really?"

Roberts said nothing.

"I'm grateful for the confidence, believe me. It's not misplaced, either. Accept my assurance of that too."

"My name is Roberts, not Shylock. I told you before I am American born, of American parents."

"I beg your pardon," abjectly. The red had left Randall's face and in its place, as on a mirror, was forming another look, of comprehension—and more. "Yet you—advised; and if not that—" of a sudden he got to his feet. Something was coming he knew to a certainty—something unexpected, vital—and he felt better able so to meet it. "Just what did you mean?"

Roberts was studying him deliberately, with the peculiar analytical look Armstrong of old had known so well.

"You can't imagine yet," he queried, "not with the motive you fancied eliminated?"

"You wish to do me a kindness, a disinterested kindness. For what reason?"

"Cut out my motive, providing I have one, for the present. It's immaterial."

"That doesn't help—I can't conceive—" On a sudden came a flash of light that augmented to a blaze. "Can it concern Margery and me? Is that it?"

Roberts did not look up. "Yes," he said.

"You know, then," tensely. "How much?"

"Everything." Roberts inspected the wall-paper opposite as though interested. "If you'll permit me I'll help you to avoid an action for divorce." A pause. "One, moreover, I can't help but feel somewhat justified."

For long, very long, there was silence absolute. Then, adequate time having passed, apparently Roberts lost interest in the wall pattern.

"Sit down, please," he suggested. "At last it seems we understand each other. Let's talk things over a bit."

CHAPTER III

FRIENDSHIP

"Very well, I'm listening."

It had come about, that return of composure, more quickly than a stranger would have thought possible, perhaps more quickly than the visitor had expected. At least for a moment he did not follow the obvious lead.

"Particularly I'm waiting for an explanation of that word 'justified' you used." The voice this time was low. "You recall you said 'justifiable action,' do you not?"

"Somewhat justifiable, yes."

Randall looked straight before him.

"Don't you agree with me?" added Roberts.

"Frankly, no. I admit I'm biassed, however—at least I trust I'm not a cad, unable to acknowledge a deficiency when shown."

"Or to administer the remedy, providing that remedy is proved innocuous?"

"Yes; I trust that also."

"Very well, we'll return to 'justifiable' qualified. It will make things easier perhaps. You don't wonder how I happen to know about your trouble?"

"There could be only one explanation."

"Thank you. That simplifies matters also." A halt; then the fundamental question direct: "Will you trust me to help you, trust me unqualifiedly?"

"Yes," no hesitation, no amplification, just that single word, "yes."

Darley Roberts remained for a moment quite still.

"Thank you, again," he said. "I have had few compliments in my life, and that is one." Again he sat quite still, all but the great hands, the only feature of him that ever showed restlessness or rebellion. "To begin with," he resumed suddenly, "I am a lawyer, not a preacher. My business is with marriage the contract, not marriage the sacrament. Sentiment has no place in law. Contracts are promises to deliver certain tangible considerations; otherwise there would be none. Again contracts are specified or implied; but morally equally binding, equally inviolable. In the eye of the law when you married Margery Cooper you contracted, by implication, to deliver certain considerations, chief among them one purely psychological — happiness. By implication you did this. Is it not so?"

"Yes, by implication."

"Have you fulfilled that contract?"

"I have tried."

"The law does not recognize attempts. We're ignoring the Church and sentiment now. Have you fulfilled your contract?"

"No; I failed."

"You admit it freely?"

"Yes; I can't do otherwise."

"Let's drop the legal point of view then. You know why you failed?"

"Yes, and no. A contract carries a mutual obligation. Margery failed also."

Roberts flashed a look.

"Do you desire a separation, too?" incisively.

"No, God, no!" It was sudden panic. "I love her."

"And she loves you," evenly. "She'll return, unquestionably — and in the future will go again as inevitably, unless you fulfil your contract. It's life."

Again Harry Randall stared straight before him, the weight of the universe suddenly on his shoulders.

"Fulfill—" he halted. "Supposing I can't fulfill?"

"Wait. We'll discuss that in a moment. First, you admit there was a certain justification for what she has done?"

No rebellion this time, no false pride.

"Yes," simply; "you were right. I admit it."

"The contract of implied happiness then; you failed because—"

Randall completed the sentence as was intended. "Because we could not live, cannot live, as Margery demands, upon what it is possible for me to make. There is absolutely no other reason."

"She is extravagant, you think?"

"For the wife of one in my position, yes."

"I didn't ask you that. Is she extravagant, for herself as she is?"

Against his will the first suggestion of color showed on Randall's face.

"I fail to see the distinction," he said.

"In other words," remorselessly, "you question my right to wield the probe. You prefer not to be hurt even to effect a cure."

"No, I repeat that I'm not a cad. Besides, I've told you I trust you. When a woman marries a man, though, with her eyes open—" He caught himself. "Pardon me, I'm ashamed to have said that. To answer your question: no; Margery wasn't extravagant in the least by her standard."

"You mean by 'her standard,'" apparently Roberts had heard only the last sentence, "the habit and experience of her whole life, of twenty-two years of precedent when you married her."

"Yes."

"And of generations of inheritance back of that. The Coopers are an old stock and have always been moderately wealthy, have they not?"

"Yes, back as far as the record goes."

"Very good. Can you, by any stretch of the imagination, fancy Mrs. Randall, being as she is, ever living happily in an atmosphere so different from that she has known, which time and circumstance have made her own? Can you?"

"No." The voice was low again, very low. "In my sane moments, never."

Roberts waited deliberately, until the pause added emphasis; with equal deliberation he drove the wedge home.

"And still, in the fulness of this knowledge, you contracted by implication to deliver to her this same thing—happiness," he said.

A second Harry Randall waited, then unconsciously he passed his hand across his face.

"Yes," he echoed, "in the fulness of knowledge I did it. I loved her."

"Loved? And yet you sacrificed her! And on top of that again labelled her rebellion unjustified!" He was silent.

Again Harry Randall's hand passed across his face, and this time it came back damp.

"God, you're hard on me!" he said. "I deserve it, though, and more. She was ignorant absolutely of what it meant to count pennies and deny herself. She couldn't realize, couldn't!"

Roberts said nothing. The leaven was working.

"I hoped, deluded myself with the belief, that it would be different; yet from the first I knew better. I was to blame absolutely. I simply loved her, as I do now—that was all."

"Yes." This time the voice was gentle, unbelievably gentle. "I think I understand—think I do. Anyway," the voice was matter of fact again, startlingly, perhaps intentionally, so, "we're wandering from the point. The past is dead. Let's bury it and look into the future. Do you see the solution yet?"

Randall looked up swiftly. He smiled; the smile of a noncombatant.

"Yes, I see it; I can't help seeing it; but—" The sentence completed itself in a gesture of impotency confessed.

"Don't do that, don't!" The annoyance was not simulated. "It's unforgivable.... You're healthy, are you not?"

"Yes."

"And strong?"

"Reasonably."

"Well, what more can you ask? The world's full of work; avalanches of it, mountains of it. It seems as though there never was so much to be done as now, to-day; and the world will pay, pay if you'll do it. Can't you see light?"

Randall caught himself in time to prevent a second gesture.

"No, frankly, I can't. I've tried, but I'm fundamentally incapable."

Roberts' great fighting face flashed about.

"You've tried—how?"

Randall hesitated, and once again the color mounted his cheek.

"I do my work here in the department the best I can, creditably, I think; but still there isn't much to look forward to, nothing adequate."

"And that's as far as you've tried?"

"Yes; I have no other training."

Roberts looked at him, merely looked.

"No other training!... You fancy this little university, this little bounded, contracted circle, is the world? You've tried! Let me see your hands."

Higher and higher mounted the tell-tale color; obedient as a schoolboy Randall obeyed. Something compelled.

Again Roberts looked and turned away. "A woman's hands; I fancied so.... And you hoped to fulfil your contract, defied fate—with those hands!" His own worked, and under command went still. "You agreed to let me help you, did you not?" he digressed suddenly.

"Yes."

"And promised to trust me? I wish that understood clearly in the beginning."

"Yes," again.

"Very well, then, that brings us back to the starting-point. I repeat my proposal that Mrs. Randall and you change your residence immediately. Must I analyze further?"

"No, I understand—and appreciate. I accept too if Margery—" he halted with a wry smile. "Do you think she—would if I asked her?"

Roberts' expression did not alter. "Supposing you write her and find out," he suggested. "And in the meantime you'll have three days to settle in your new home," he added irrelevantly.

Again Randall colored, like a youth planning on building his first nest. The contagion of the thing was upon him, the infinite, rosy possibilities manifest.

"I can do it easily," he said, "and she'll be surprised—and pleased—I can fancy the way she'll look now." Second thought intruded. "I'm afraid, though, the few things we've got here won't even make an impression there. The place is so big by comparison."

"That's all right," easily. "I said I'd want to take a hand." He had a seeming inspiration. "Supposing you get Miss Gleason to help you and suggest what more is needed. I'm sure she'd do it for Mrs. Randall and you. I'll speak to her too."

"Just the thing. I'd like that immensely. No one can help that way like Elice."

"Let's consider it settled then." His point carried, Roberts' great hands were loose in his lap again. "I had just one other matter I wished to speak about to-night. How'd you like to accept a position under me with the new company?" He did not elaborate this time, did not dissimulate. "I'll personally guarantee you four thousand a year, beginning January first, with three weeks' vacation."

"How would I like it!" For the third time Harry Randall fell to polishing his glasses; but this time, in spite of an effort to prevent, his hand shook visibly. "You don't need to ask me that. It would be a miracle; only — only I'm a bit afraid of a position of that kind — afraid it would be too big."

"The company would expect you to earn it, of course," impassively.

"But I'm not worth it. I know that and I don't want to accept under false representations. It's beyond me."

"Beyond nothing!" curtly. "If I say you're worth it, you are. I'll make you so — help if necessary. Do you accept?"

"Accept, yes, and thank you. I won't protest, or presume to misunderstand your intent in offering it to me. I realize you're giving me a chance to make good where I failed to fulfil my obligation with Margery." The voice was not so steady as it might have been and for an instant Randall halted. "If you don't mind, though," he went on, "I'd like to ask you a question. I can't conceive why you, a stranger, practically, should do all this for me. I'm simply confused, it's all so unprecedented. Why do you do it, please?"

Into Darley Roberts' eyes crept the old odd smile that spread no farther.

"You mean it's all so unprecedented — of me," he returned bluntly.

Randall said nothing. It was true.

"Wasn't that what you meant?" he repeated, and just for a second the smile crept beyond the eyes.

"Yes. It's useless to lie."

"—To me?"

This time Randall's face flamed undeniably.

"Yes—to you," he admitted. "You're positively uncanny."

"Don't do it then," shortly, "ever. To answer your question: The main reason, I think, is because to-day is December the sixth—a holiday."

"A holiday!" Randall stared, as in the morning Herbert had stared.

"With me.... Another reason is that I've been an under dog myself for a very long time and—perhaps, though, I am mistaken."

"No, I'm one of the breed unquestionably."

"And under dogs have a fondness for each other instinctively."

Randall held his peace. He had the quality of presentiment and it was active now.

"There was still a third reason." No smile in the blue eyes now, just an impassive blank. "I had a call a few days ago from an upper dog, by heredity. He offered me a thousand dollars cold not to do—what I've just done."

Randall was not a good gambler. His face whitened to the lips.

"You refer to Margery's father," he said.

"Yes. It seemed to me well, under the circumstances, for you to know. He was strongly in favor of letting matters drift. I gathered he has never been particularly fond of you."

"No, never. But Margery—"

"I understand absolutely. Take this for what it is worth from a disinterested observer: Your wife is square, man, from the ground up. Don't ever for an instant, because you were reared differently and have a different point of view, fancy otherwise. Tote your end of the load fair—I believe you see how now—and she'll tote hers. It'll be worth your while."

"Roberts!" Randall was upon his feet, he could not do otherwise. "Honestly I don't know how to thank you. Anything that I can say, can do even—"

"Don't try, please. I'd rather you wouldn't." No pretence in that frank aversion, no affectation. He arose as one whose labor is over. "Let it go at that."

In sheer perplexity Randall frowned. His hands sought his pockets.

"But, confound it, I don't like to. It's so inhumanly ungrateful." The frown deepened. "Besides, when this intoxication is off I'll realize what a lot I'm accepting from you. That house, for instance. You didn't buy a place of that kind for an investment or for yourself alone. I'm not an absolute ass. You'll want it all some of these times, and then—"

Slowly Roberts faced about; equally slowly he smiled.

"Would it relieve your mind any," he finally asked, "if I were to promise to tell you the moment I do want it—all?"

"Yes, a lot."

"I give you my word then."

"Thanks. I believe that too; but—"

For the second time Roberts smiled, the smile of finality unquestionable.

"Must we return and go through it all again?" he asked. "It's after midnight now, but if you wish—"

"No; not that either."

"All right. I'll send the office-boy around in the morning to help you move. He has nothing else really to do." Roberts paused at a sudden thought. "By the way, I'll not be back until a week from to-morrow. Suppose we have a little housewarming, just we four—strangers, that night?" and before the other could answer, before the complex suggestion in its entirety took effect, he was gone.

CHAPTER IV

COMPREHENSION

It was three o'clock in the afternoon of a sultry July Sunday when a big red roadster drew up all but noiselessly and, with an instinct common to all motorists, a heritage from an equine age past, stopped at the nose of the hitching-post in front of the Gleason cottage. In it the single occupant throttled down the engine until it barely throbbed. Alighting, goggles on forehead, he passed up the walk toward the house. Not until he was fairly at the steps did he apparently notice his surroundings. Then, unexpectedly, he bared his head.

"Be not surprised, it is I," he said. "Not in the spirit alone but in the flesh." Equally without warning he smiled. "Needless to say I'm glad to see you again, Elice," as he took the girl's offered hand. Then deliberately releasing it: "and you too, Armstrong," extending his own.

Precisely as, with his companion of the shady porch, he had risen upon the newcomer's advent, the other man stood there. If possible his face, already unnaturally pale for a torrid afternoon, shaded whiter as an instant passed without his making a motion in response.

"And you too, Armstrong," Roberts repeated, the smile still on his face, the hand still extended; then, when there still came no response, the voice lowered until it was just audible, but nevertheless significant in its curt brevity: "Shake whether you want to or not. There are seven pairs of eyes watching from behind that trellis across the street."

Armstrong obeyed as though moved by a wire.

"Speak loud, so they can all hear. They're listening too," directed the low-voiced mentor.

Armstrong, red in the face now, formulated the conventional.

"Thanks." Roberts sat down on the top step, his big-boned body at ease, his great bushy head, in which the gray was beginning to sprinkle thick, a contrast to the dark pillar of the porch. "I just returned an hour ago," he added as casually as though food for gossip had not been avoided by a hair's breadth and was not still imminent. "It's good, unqualifiedly, to be back."

Armstrong returned to his seat, a bit uncertainly. His hands were trembling uncontrollably; in self-defence he thrust them deep into his pockets.

"Have you been out of town?" he asked.

"Yes, for over a month." No affectation in that even friendliness. He laughed suddenly in tolerant, all but impersonal, self-analysis. "And I'm tired—tired until the marrow of my bones aches." He laughed again. "It seems as though I never was so tired in my life."

Armstrong looked at him, in a sudden flash of the old confidence and admiration.

"I beg your pardon, then," he said hurriedly. "I didn't know that you had been away, of course, and rather fancied, from your coming so unexpected—And that again after two years almost—You can understand how it was possible, can't you? I'm ashamed."

"Certainly I can understand," easily. "Let's all forget it. I have already." He smiled an instant comprehensively fair into the blue eyes, then characteristically abruptly he digressed. "By the way, Elice," he said, "can't we have some of those cookies of yours? I've dreamed of them, along with other things, until—Do, please, if they're in stock. I mean it. Still down at Phelps's are you?" he asked the other directly when the girl had gone.

"No." A long pause wherein Armstrong did not look up. "I—left there a couple of weeks ago. I'm not doing anything in particular just now."

The cookies, far-famed and seemingly always available, were on hand, and Roberts relapsed into silence. From her own seat behind them Elice Gleason sat looking at the two men, precisely as she had looked that first evening they had called in company.

"That's a new motor out there, isn't it?" she asked at last.

"Yes." Roberts roused and shook the scattered crumbs off his khaki coat. "It came while I was away. This is the first try-out."

Miss Gleason was examining the big machine with a critical eye. "This is a six-cylinder, I judge. What's become of the old four, Old—"

"Reliable?"

"Yes."

"Disgraced its name." Roberts smiled peculiarly. "I took it along with me when I went West. It's scrapped out there on the Nevada desert, God knows where, thirty miles from nowhere. I fancy the vultures are wondering right now what in the world it is."

"You had an accident?"

"Rather." Roberts got to his feet deliberately. "Some other time I'll tell you the story, if you wish. It would take too long now, and it's entirely too hot here." He looked at his two listeners impartially. "Besides, there's other business more urgent. I have a curiosity to see how quickly the six-eighty out there will eat up thirty miles. It's guaranteed to do it in twenty-five minutes. Won't you come along?

"I'll take the rumble and you two sit forward," he added as they hesitated. "You can drive as well as I can, Elice."

"Not to-day; some other time," declined Armstrong, hurriedly. He started up to avoid a change of purpose, and to cover any seeming precipitancy lit a cigarette with deliberation. "I was going, really, anyway."

Roberts did not insist, nor did he dissimulate.

"As you wish. I meant it or I shouldn't have made the suggestion. Better glue on your hair if you accept, Elice. I have a presentiment that I'll let her out to-day." He started down the walk. "I'm ready when you are."

Behind him the man and the girl exchanged one look.

"Come, Steve," said the girl in a low voice. "I ask it."

"No," Armstrong's thin face formed a smile, a forced, crooked smile; "I meant what I said, too, or I wouldn't have refused. Likewise I also have a presentiment—of a different kind. Good-bye."

"Steve!"

"No."

And that was all.

Out in the long street, University Row, glided the big red roadster; slowly through the city limits, more rapidly through the suburbs, then, as the open country beyond came to view, it began gradually to find itself.

"Want to see her go, do you, Elice?" asked Roberts, as the town behind them grew indistinct in a fog of dust.

"Yes, if you wish."

"If I wish." Roberts brought the goggles down from his forehead significantly. "If I wish," he repeated, the inflection peculiar. He looked ahead. The broad prairie road, dust white in its July whiteness, stretched straight out before them, without a turn or a curve, direct as the crow flies for forty miles, and on through two counties, as he knew. A light wind, begot of their motion alone, played on their faces, mingled with the throbbing purr of the engine in their ears. "If I wish," for the third time; and notch by notch the throttle began to open.

On they went, the self-evolved breeze a gale now, the throb of the big motor a continuous moan, the cloud of dust behind them a dull brown bank against the sky. On they went over convex grades that tilted gently first to the right, then to the left, over culverts that spoke one single note of protest, over tiny bridges that echoed hollow at the impact; past dazzling green cornfields and yellow blocks of ripening grain, through great shadows of homestead groves and clumps of willows that marked the lowest point of swales, on—on—

Roberts leaned over close, but his eyes did not leave the road for the fraction of a second.

"Afraid, girl?" he asked.

"No."

Again the man looked ahead. They were fair in the open now, already far from the city. It was the heat of a blistering Sunday and not a team or a pedestrian was astir. Ahead, for a mile, for miles perhaps, as far as they could see, not an animate dot marred the surface of the taut, stretched, yellow-white ribbon.

"Shall I let her out, Elice?"

"Yes."

"Sure you're not afraid—in the least?"

"Certain."

Again the throttle lever and its companion spark began to move around the tiny sextant, approaching nearer and nearer. Simultaneously, sympathetic, as though actuated by the same power, the hand of the speedometer on the dash began to crawl up and up. They had been all but racing before; but now—

Behind them the cloud of dust rose higher and higher, and darker and darker as the suction increased. To either side was no longer yellow and green distinct, but a mingling, indistinct, mottled unreality. Ahead the ribbon of yellow and white seemed to rise up and throw itself into their faces; again and again endlessly. The engine no longer moaned. It roared as a fire under draft. The wind was a wall that held them back like a vise in their places. In the flash of a glance the man looked at the face of the dial. The single arm was pasted black over the numeral sixty. Once more the throttle advanced a notch, the spark lever two—and the hand halted at sixty-five. The wind gripped them afresh, and like human fingers grappled with them. Up, fairly level with their eyes, lifted the advancing yellow-white ribbon. By his side, though he did not look, the man knew that the girl had covered her face with her hands, was struggling against the gale to breathe. He was struggling himself, through wide-opened nostrils, his lips locked tight. On his bare hands the sweat gushed forth and, despite the suction, glistened bright. Yet once more, the last time the throttle moved, the spark— and met on the sextant. With its last ounce of power the great car responded, thrilled; one could feel it, a vital thing. Once again the speed-hand on the indicator stirred; but this time the man did not see it, dared not look even for the fraction of a second. Like grim death, grim life, he clung to the wheel; his eyes not on the road beneath but a quarter of a mile ahead. About him the scuttling earth shaded from motley to gray; but he did not see. A solitary tree loomed ahead beside the ribbon, and seemed to crack like a rifle report as they flashed past. At the radiator vent a tiny cloud of steam arose, caught the gale, and stung damp on his cheeks. Far ahead, then nearer and nearer miraculously, a blot of green that he knew was the tree fringe of a river, took form, swept forward to meet them, came nearer and nearer, arose like a wall—

Back into neutral, separating until they were once more opposite, went the two companions of the sextant. Simultaneously again the speed indicator followed the backward trail. Incredibly swift the gale dwindled, until it barely fanned their cheeks. The roar of the great engine subsided, until once more it was a gentle murmur. The vivid green and the dull yellow of summer took their respective places; and like a live thing, beaten and cowed, the big car drew up at the very edge of the grove, left the yellow road-ribbon, rustled a moment amid the half-parched grass and halted in the shadow blot of a big water maple—thirty miles almost to a rod from the city limits they had left.

A moment the two humans in the seat remained in their places, breathing hard. Deliberately, almost methodically, Roberts wiped the sweat from his face.

"Thirty-two minutes, the clock says," he commented. "We dawdled though at first. At the finish—" He looked at the indicator peculiarly. "I'd really like to have known, for sure."

The girl stood up. She trembled a little.

"Would you really? Perhaps—"

"You looked, Elice? I fancied you shut your eyes."

"I did—only for a second. It read seventy-two."

Roberts turned a switch and the last faint purr ceased.

"I imagined, almost, you'd be afraid," he said evenly.

"I was—horribly," simply.

"You were; and still—I won't do it again, Elice."

Without a word the girl stepped to the ground. In equal silence the man followed. Taking off the long khaki coat he spread it on the ground amid the shadow and indicated his handiwork with a nod. For a half-minute perhaps he himself remained standing, however, his great shoulders squared, his big fingers twitching unconsciously. Recollecting, he dropped on the grass beside her.

"Pardon me, Elice," he apologized bluntly, "for frightening you." He smiled, the infrequent, tolerant, self-analytic smile. "I somehow couldn't help doing what I did. I knew it would break out sometime soon. I couldn't help it."

For a moment the girl inspected him, her head, just lifted, resting on her locked arms, her eyelids half closed.

"You knew—what? Something's happened I know; something unusual, very. I never saw you before as you are to-day. I'd almost say you had nerves. Do you care to tell me?"

Roberts was still smiling.

"Do you care to have me tell you?" he countered.

"Yes, if you wish."

"If I wish—if I wish—you told me that once before, you recall."

"Yes."

"And I proceeded to frighten you—horribly. You said so."

"Yes," again.

"Does that mean you wish to be frightened again? Do you enjoy it?"

"Enjoy it? I don't know. I'm curious to listen, if you care to tell me."

Roberts had stretched himself luxuriously on the cool sod. He looked up steadily, through the tangled leaves, at the dotted blue beyond.

"There's nothing to frighten you this time," he said. "Nothing to tell much, just—money."

"I gathered as much."

"And why, Elice?"

"Several reasons. First of all, a practical man doesn't carry an automobile half across the continent by express without a definite stake involved. Later he doesn't 'scrap,' as you say, that same machine without regret unless the stake was big—and won."

"You think I won, then?"

"I know."

"And again, why?"

The girl flashed a glance, but he was not looking at her.

"Because you always win," she said simply.

"Always?" A pause. "Always, Elice?"

"Always in matters of—money."

The man lay there still, looking up. Barely a leaf in the big maple was astir, not a single sensate thing. Had they been the only two people alive on a desert expanse they could not have been more isolated, more completely alone. Yet he pursued the lead no further, neither by word nor suggestion. Creeping through a tiny gap a ray of sunlight glared in his eyes, and he shifted enough to avoid it. That was all.

In her place the girl too shifted, just so she could see him more distinctly.

"Tell me about it," she said. "I'm listening."

"You're really interested? I don't care to bore you."

"Yes, really. I never pretend with you."

Slowly Roberts sat up, his head bare, his fingers locked over his knees.

"Very well. I 'phoned, you remember, that I was going West to look at a mining claim."

"Yes."

"What I should have said, to be exact, was that I was going to file on one, if it wasn't too late. I'd already seen it, on paper, and ore from it; had it assayed myself. It ran above two hundred dollars. It was one of those things that happen outside of novels oftener than people imagine. The man who furnished the specimens was named Evans,—a big, raw-boned cowboy I met down in the Southwest, where I've got an interest in a silver mine. He'd contracted the fever and worked for our company for a time. When the Nevada craze came on he got restless and wanted to go too. He hadn't a second shirt to his back so I grub-staked him. Nothing came of it and I staked him again. This time he came here personally to report. He had some ore with him and a map; just that and nothing more. Whether he'd found anything worth while he didn't know, didn't imagine he had, as it was a new section that hadn't produced as yet. He hadn't even taken the trouble to secure his claim. What he wanted was more money, grub money; and he had brought the specimen along as a teaser. He swore he hadn't mentioned the matter to a soul except me. There wasn't any hurry either, he said, or danger. The prospect was forty miles out on the desert from Tonopah, no railroad nearer, and no one was interested there much as yet. If I'd advance him another thousand, though—I'd been backing him a thousand dollars at a time—he'd go back and file regular, and when I'd had an assay made, if the thing looked good, he'd sell to me outright for five thousand cash."

For the first time the speaker halted, looked at the listener directly.

"Still interested, are you?" he queried. "It's all money, money from first to last."

"Yes, go on. I think I saw this man Evans, didn't I, around with you for several days?"

"Possibly. I kept him here while I was getting a report. I'd seen some ore before and the scent looked warm to me. Besides, I knew Evans, and under the circumstances I felt better to keep him in sight. I did for a week, night and day. He never left me for an hour. He'd been eating my bread and salt for a year, had every reason to be under obligation and loyal, was so tentatively, his coming proved that; but, while one has to trust others up to a certain point in this world, beyond that—I've found beyond that it's better not to take chances, even on obligation.... Have you ever known anything of the kind yourself?"

The girl was not looking at him now. "I've had little experience with people," she evaded, "very little. Go on, please. I'm interested."

"Well, the report came the day I 'phoned you, on the last delivery. Evans was killing time, as usual, about the office and I called him into my private room and locked the door. I read it through to him aloud, every word; and, he didn't seem to take it all in at first, again. All at once the thing came over him, the full meaning of that assay of two hundred dollars to the ton—and he went to pieces, like a fly-wheel that's turned too fast. He simply caved. For ten years he'd been chasing the rainbow of chance, and now all at once, when he'd fairly given up hope, he'd stumbled upon it and the pot of gold together. It was too much for him.

"This was at five o'clock in the afternoon, I say. At six o'clock I unlocked the door and things began to move definitely. What happened in that hour doesn't matter. It wasn't pleasant, and under the circumstances no one would believe me if I told; for I had his written promise to show me the ledge he'd found and to sell whatever right he had to the claim himself to me for twenty-five thousand dollars.... I found it, I have an incontestable title to it, and I refused a million dollars flat for it less than three days ago!"

In her place the girl half raised, met the speaker eye to eye.

"And still, knowing in advance it was worth a fortune, Evans sold to you."

"Yes, voluntarily; begged it of me. I said no one would believe me now, even you—I don't care for the opinion of any one else."

"I don't doubt you, not for a second." The brown eyes had dropped now. "But I can't quite understand."

"No, I repeat once more, no one can understand who wasn't there. He was crazy, avariciously crazy. He wanted the money then, then; wanted to see it, to feel it, that minute. It was his and he wanted it; not the five thousand he'd promised, but five times that. He wouldn't wait. He would have it.

"I tried to reason with him, to argue with him, offered him his own terms if he'd let me develop it; but he wouldn't listen. If I wouldn't accept he'd throw me over entirely, notwithstanding the fact that I'd made the find possible, and sell to some one else—sell something he didn't have; for at last it all came out, why he'd gone crazy and wouldn't wait. He'd lied to me previously. Before he'd left Tonopah he'd talked, told of his find to a half-dozen of his friends, and left them specimens of the same ore he'd brought me. He'd told them everything, in fact, except the location. It developed that he had retained judgment enough to keep back even a hint of that; and they were waiting for him there,—he knew it and I knew it,—waiting his

144

return, waiting to learn the location, and to steal his claim before he could stake it himself."

"And still, feeling certain of that in your own mind, you paid him his price!"

"Every dollar of it—before I took the midnight train West. I raised it after business hours, in a dozen different ways; but I got it. I pooled for security everything I had in the world—except Old Reliable; I kept that free for a purpose,—my house, my library, my stock in the traction company, some real estate I own. I had to give good measure because I had to have the money right then. And I got it. It was a pull but I got it."

The girl's head was back on her folded arms once more, the long lashes all but covering her eyes.

"Supposing Evans had been lying to you after all," she suggested, "in other things besides the one you mentioned."

Over Roberts' face flashed a momentary smile.

"I told you we were locked in that room together for an hour. He wasn't lying to me after that time had passed, rest assured. Besides, I wasn't entirely helpless or surprised. I'd been out in that country myself and Evans wasn't the only man I had reporting. I'd been waiting for a chance of this kind from the day the first prospect developed at Goldfield. I knew it would come sometime—if I waited my chance."

"So you gambled—with every cent you had in the world."

"Yes. All life is a gamble. If I had lost I was only thirty-five and the earth is big. Besides, to all the world I was still 'old man' Roberts, not 'Darley.' There was yet plenty of time—if I lost."

"You went West that same evening, you say." The long lashes were all but touching now. "What then?"

"Yes, with Evans in the same Pullman section and Old Reliable in the express car forward. I had an idea in my head and followed it out. I felt as certain as I was of my own name that they'd have scouts out to wire ahead when Evans was coming; so it wouldn't be any use to get off at an obscure place. I also knew that the chances were I couldn't get a conveyance there at once for love or money; so Old Reliable was already—good and ready. Every tank was full. The tonneau was packed: ten gallons extra gas, five gallons of water, a week's rations—everything I could think of that we might need. We'd go through to the end of the line, all right, but if I could help it we shouldn't wait long after we got there. And we didn't."

This time the girl did not interrupt, either with comment or gesture; merely lay there listening.

"Ten minutes after we struck town we were away, under our own power. It was night, but we were away just the same. And that's where we got the lead,—a half hour's lead. They knew, all right, that we'd come, fancied they knew everything—but they hadn't planned on Old Reliable. It took them just that long to come to and make readjustment. Then the real fun began. There was no moon, and out on the desert the night was as dark as a pocket. We simply had to have a light even if it gave us away. Evans thought he knew the road; but, if there ever was one, before we'd gone ten miles we'd lost it. After that I drove by compass entirely—and instinct. But I couldn't go fast. I didn't dare to. For an hour and a half—the indicator showed we'd gone twenty-four miles—we had everything to ourselves, seemingly the entire world. We hadn't heard a sound or seen a live thing. Then, as we came up on a rise, Evans looked back and saw a light,—just one light, away, away back like a star. A few seconds afterward it disappeared and we made a couple more miles. We mounted a second rise and—this time Evans swore. He was with me by this time, body and soul, game to the finish; for the light wasn't starlike now by any means. It didn't even twinkle. It just simply rose up out of the ground, shone steady, vanished for a time, and rose up anew with the lay of the country. They were on our trail at last, they couldn't miss it. It was plain as a wagon road, and they were making two miles to our one. They must have had a good car; but anyway everything was with them. They could drive to the limit by our trail; but I couldn't, for I didn't know what was ahead. I let her out, though, and Evans watched. He didn't swear now, he just watched; and every time that light showed it was nearer. At last,—

we'd made thirty-two miles by that time,—he saw two lights behind instead of one—and saw them red, I judge, for how he swore! It was then or never and I opened the throttle to the last notch and we flew over everything, through everything until—we stopped."

"You struck something?"

"Yes. I don't know what nor didn't stop to see. The transmission went, I knew that. The engine was still threshing and pounding when we took to our heels. We could hear it and see the two lights coming and we ran—Lord, how we ran! It seems humorous now, but it wasn't humorous then. There was a fortune at stake and a big one; for a claim belongs to the chap who puts up the monuments. We ran straight ahead into the night, until we couldn't run another foot; and then we walked, walked, ten miles if an inch, until the two lights of Old Reliable became one, and then went out of sight entirely. Then we lay down and panted and waited for daylight.... That's about all, I guess."

"They didn't follow you, then?" The girl was sitting up now, the brown eyes wide open.

"They couldn't. A hound might have done so, but a human being couldn't that night." Roberts dropped back to the grass, again avoiding the rift of light. "At daylight Evans got his bearings, and that day we found the claim, built our monuments, tacked up the notice and the rest. I learned afterwards there were six men in the machine behind; but I never saw any of them—until the day I left. They made me an offer then."

"And Old Reliable?"

Roberts hesitated, then he laughed oddly.

"I paid a parting visit there too. The remains weren't decent junk when the same six got through expressing their feelings that night."

CHAPTER V

FULFILMENT

An hour had passed. As the afternoon sun sank lower the shadow blot beneath the big maple had lengthened and deepened. In consequence the annoying light-rift was no more. Overhead the leaves were vibrating, barely vibrating, with the first breath of breeze of evening born. Otherwise there was no change; just the big red roadster and the man and the girl idling beside.

"Poverty, work, subservience," conversation had drifted where it would, at last had temporarily halted, with the calendar rolled back twenty years; "poverty, work, subservience," the man had paused there to laugh, the odd, repressed laugh that added an emphasis no mere words could express. "Yes; they're old friends of mine, very old friends, very. I'm not likely to forget the contrast they've made, ever, no matter what the future holds."

"You've not forgotten, then, what's past,—overlooked it? Isn't it better to forget, sometimes,—some things?"

"Forget?" The man was looking straight up into space. "I wish I could forget, wish it from the bottom of my soul. It makes me—hard at times, and I don't want to be hard. But I can't ever. Memory is branded in too deeply."

The girl was picking a blade of grass to pieces, bit by bit.

"I'm disappointed. I fancied you could do anything you wished," she said low. "That's what has made me afraid of you sometimes."

The man did not stir.

"Are you afraid of me sometimes, really?" he asked.

"Yes, horribly—as much afraid as when we were coming out here to-day."

"I'm sorry, Elice, sorry for several reasons. Most of all because I love you."

It was the first word of the kind that had ever passed between them. Yet neither showed surprise, nor did either change position. It was as though he had said that gravitation makes the apple fall, or that the earth was round, a thing they had both known for long, had become instinctively adjusted to.

"I knew that," said the girl gently, "and know too that you're sorry I am afraid. You can't help it. If it weren't true, though, you wouldn't be you."

The man looked at her gravely.

"You think it will always be that way?" he asked. "You'll always be afraid at times, I mean?"

"Yes. You're bigger than I am. I can't understand you, I never can wholly. I've given up hope. We're all afraid of things we can't completely understand."

Silently the man passed his hand across his face, unconsciously; his arm fell lax at his side. As the girl had known, he did not follow the lead, would not follow it unless she directed the way.

"You said you fancied I could forget what's past," he said at last. "Did you honestly believe that?"

"Yes, or ignore it."

"Ignore it—or forget!" The fingers of the great hands twitched. "Some things one can't ignore or forget, girl. To do so would be superhuman. You don't understand."

"No; you've never told me. You've suggested at times, merely suggested; nothing more."

"You'd like to know why—the reason? It would help you to understand?"

"Yes; I think it would help."

"It might even lead to making you—unafraid?"

A halt this time, then, "Yes, it might possibly do even that."

Again the man looked at her for long in silence, and again very gravely.

"I'll tell you, then," he said. "It isn't pleasant for me to tell nor for you to hear; but I'd like you to know why—if you can. They're all back, back, the things I'd like to forget and can't, a very long way. They date from the time I first knew anything."

The girl settled deeper into the soft coat, her eyes half closed.

"You told me once you couldn't remember your mother even," she suggested.

"No, nor my father, nor any other relatives, if I ever had any. I was simply stranded in Kansas City when it was new. I wasn't born there, though, but out West on a prairie ranch somewhere. The tradition is that my parents were hand-to-mouth theatrical people, who'd got the free home craze and tried to live out on the west Kansas desert, who were dried out and starved out until they went back on the road; and who then, of course, didn't want me. I don't know. Anyway, when my brain awoke I was there in Kansas City. As a youngster I had a dozen homes—and none. I was any one's property—and no one's. I did anything, accepted whatever Providence offered, to eat. Animals must live and I was no exception. The hand seemingly of every man and woman in the world was against me, and I conformed to the inevitable. Any one weaker than I was my prey, any one stronger my enemy. I learned to fight for my own, to run when it was wisest, to take hard knocks when I couldn't avoid them—and say nothing. It was all in the game. I know this isn't pleasant to hear," he digressed.

"I'm listening. Go on, please."

"That was the first stage. Then, together with a hundred other similar little beasts, a charitable organization got hold of me and transplanted me out into the country, as they do old footsore hack horses when they get to cluttering the pavement. Chance ordained that I should draw an old Norwegian farmer, the first generation over, and that he should draw me. I fancy we were equally pleased. His contract was to feed me and clothe me and, —I was twelve at the time, by the way,—to get out of me in return what work he could. There was no written contract, of course; but nevertheless it was understood just the same.

"He fulfilled his obligation—in his way. He was the first generation over, I repeat, and had no more sense of humor than a turtle. He saw that I had all I could eat—after I'd done precisely so much work, his own arbitrary stint, and not a minute before. If I was one iota short I went hungry as an object-lesson. He gave me clothes to wear, after every other member of the family had discarded them, in supreme disregard for suitability or fit. He sent me to school—during the months of January and February, when there was absolutely nothing else to do, and when I should have been in the way at home. At times of controversy he was mighty with the rod. He was, particularly at the beginning of our intimacy, several sizes larger than I. It was all a very pleasant arrangement, and lasted four years. It ended abruptly one Thanksgiving Day.

"I remember that day distinctly, as much so as yesterday. Notwithstanding it was a holiday, I'd been husking corn all day steady, from dark until dark. There was snow on the ground, and I came in wet through, chattering cold, hungry, and dog-tired—to find the entire family had left to celebrate the evening with a neighbor. They did that often of a holiday, but usually they left word. This time they'd forgotten, or didn't care. Anyway, it didn't matter, for that day had been the last straw. So far as I was concerned the clock had struck twelve and a new circuit had begun.

"I looked about the kitchen for supper, but there was none, so I proceeded to prepare one suitable to the occasion. Among other things, the farmer raised turkeys for the market and, although the season was late, there were a few birds left for seed. I went out to the barn with a lantern and picked the plumpest gobbler I could find off the roost, and an hour later had him in the oven. This was at eight o'clock in the evening. While he was baking I canvassed the old farmer's wardrobe. I'd grown like a mushroom those last years and, though I was only sixteen, a suit of his ready-made clothes was a fair fit. I got into it grimly. I also found a dog-skin fur coat and, while it smelled a good deal like its original owner, it would be warm, and I laid it aside carefully for future reference.

"Then came supper. I didn't hurry in the least, but I had a campaign in mind, so I went to work. When that bird was done I ate it, and everything else I could find. I had the appetite of an ostrich, and when I was through there wasn't enough left for a hungry cat. I even considered taking the family cat in to the feast,—they had one, of course, and it always looked hungry, too; but I had a sort of pride in my achievement and I wanted to leave the remains as evidence.

"It was ten o'clock by this time and no one had shown up. I was positively sorry. I'd hoped the old farmer would return and find me. I had a few last words to say to him, some that had been lying heavy on my mind for a long time. But he didn't come, and I couldn't wait any longer; so I wrote them instead. I put on the dog-skin coat and started away on foot into the night. If I'd had money I would have left the value of the clothes; but he'd never given me a dollar in all those four years, so I took them on account. It was two miles to town and I made it in time to catch the ten-forty-five freight out.

"I forgot one thing, though. I went back after I'd got started a quarter of a mile to say good-bye to the horses. I always liked horses, and old Bill and Jerry and I had been good friends. I rode the pilot of that engine and got into Kansas City the next morning. That was the second stage.... Still interested, are you, Elice?"

"Yes."

"Next, I landed in the hardwood region of Missouri, the north edge of the Ozarks. It was the old story of one having to live, and I'd seen an ad in the papers for 'loggers wanted.' I had answered it, and the man in charge dropped on me like a hawk and gave me transportation by the first train. Evidently men for the job were not in excess, and when I'd been there a day I knew why. It was the most God-forsaken country I'd ever known, away back in the mountains, where civilization had ceased advancing fifty years before. The job was a contract to deliver so many thousand feet of lumber in the log daily at the mill on the nearest railway. There was a five-mile haul, and we worked under a boss in crews of four. Each crew had to deliver eight big logs a day, seven days in the week, three hundred and sixty-five days in the year. How it was done, when they were cut, when hauled, was not the boss's affair—just so the logs came. When we of the crews ate or slept was no one's affair—just so we kept on the job. No single man could handle one of those big cuts, no single mule team haul it in places over those cursed mountain roads. That's why we worked in crews. On the average we worked eighteen hours a day. In summer this was long, in winter it seemed perpetual; but I was in it and I was going to stick—or thought I was. The other three in my gang were middle-aged men,—hard drinkers, good swearers, tough as oak themselves. The boss was a little tobacco-eating, bow-legged Irishman. I never, before or since, knew a man who could swear as he could, or drink so when he struck town. It seems to go with the logging business; but he was a master.

"I struck this place in the winter. It was in the winter following, again by chance on a holiday, but Christmas this time, that I quit. They don't have much cold down in that country and usually but little snow; but this year there had been a lot,—soft, wet snow, half rain, that melted on the ground and made the roads almost impassable. For that reason we'd been getting behind in our contract. We simply could not make two trips a day; and Murphy, the boss, grew black and blacker. He swore that if we couldn't make but one trip a day on that one haul we'd have to carry two logs each instead of one. The thing was barely possible on good roads, wholly impossible with the ground softened; but he was the boss, his word law, and before daylight on this Christmas morning we were loaded and on the road.

"I was on the head wagon with Murphy behind me, the other three following. The first half-mile was down grade and we got along all right. Then came the inevitable up grade following and the team began to flounder. They were mules, of course,—horses could never have stood for a day the grief of that mountain hauling,—great big-framed, willing fellows that in condition would pull anything any team could pull; but now they were weak and tired, and so thin that their bones almost stuck through their hides from the endless grind.

They did their best, though, and struggled along for a few rods. The wheels struck a rock in the road and they stopped. I urged them on and they tried again, but the load wouldn't budge. There was but one thing to do,—to double with the team behind, and I slid off to make the coupling.

"Murphy had been watching it all in silence,—a bad sign with him. When he saw what I was going to do he held up his hand to the rear team, which meant:'Stay where you are.' 'Give over the lines,' he said to me.

"I knew what that meant. I'd seen him cripple animals before; but that was when I first came. Since then I'd had another year to grow and to get hard and tough. I was going on eighteen and as big as I am now almost; and I wasn't afraid of him then or of any human being alive.

"'It's no use,' I answered. 'We may as well double and save time.'

"He said something then, no matter what; I was used to being sworn at.

"'No,' I said.

"He jumped off the load at that. I thought it was between us, so I jerked off my big mittens to be ready; but the mules' turn was to come first, it seems. He didn't wait for anything, just simply went at them, like a maniac, like a demon. I won't tell you about it—it was too horribly brutal—or about what followed. I simply saw red. For the first time and the last time in my life, I hope, I fought a man— fought like a beast, tooth and nail. When it was over he was lying there in the mud we'd made, unconscious; and I was looking down at him and gasping for breath. I was bleeding in a dozen places, for he had a knife; but I never noticed. I suppose I stood there so for a minute looking at him, the other three men who had come up looking at me, and not one of us saying a word. I reached over and felt of him from head to foot. There were no bones broken and he was breathing steadily. So I did what I suppose was a cruel thing, but one I've never regretted to this day, though I've never seen him since. I simply rolled him over and over in the mud and slush out of the road—and left him to come to. After that we pulled off the second log from each of the four wagons and left them there beside the track. Then we drove on to town, leaving him there; sitting up by that time, still dazed, by the side of the road. There was just one logging train a day on that stub, and when we pulled into town it was waiting. Without a word of understanding, or our pay for the month, the four of us took that train and went our four separate ways. That's the third stage.... Begin to understand a little, do you, Elice?"

"Yes; I begin, just begin, to understand—many things."

Roberts shifted position silently, his arms crossed under his head for a pillow. But he was still looking straight up, through the gently rocking leaves at the infinite beyond.

"The next stage found me in a southern Iowa soft-coal mine. The explanation is simple. I had saved a few dollars; while they lasted I drifted, and to the north. When they were gone I had to work or starve. I had no education whatever, no special training even. I was merely a big, healthy animal, fit only for hard, physical work. I happened to be in a farming and mining community. It was Winter and there was nothing to do on a farm, so by the law of necessity I went to work heaving coal.

"I stayed there a little over seven months and during that time I scarcely saw the sun. I'd go into the tunnel at seven in the morning, take my lunch with me, and never come out until quitting time. I worked seven days in the week here too. There wasn't any union and, anyway, no one seemed to think of doing differently. At first it used to worry me, that being always in the dark. My imagination kept working, picturing sunlight and green things; after a bit that stage passed and I used to dread to come out of the tunnel. The glare hurt my eyes and made me blink like an owl in the daytime. I felt chilly, too, and shivered so my teeth chattered. But I stuck to it, and after a few months the thing seemed natural and almost as though I'd been there always. I began to cease to think and to work unconsciously, like a piece of machinery. I even quit counting the days. They were all the same, so what was the use? I just worked,

worked, and the coal dust ground into me and sweated into me until I looked more like a negro than a white man.

"Time drifted on this way, from Winter until Spring, from Spring until Summer; at last the something unusual that always comes about sooner or later happened, and I awoke. It was just after dinner one day and I'd gone back to the job. I had a lot of loose coal knocked down in the drift and was shovelling steadily into a car when, away down the main tunnel, I saw a bunch of lights bobbing in the darkness. It wasn't the time of day for an inspection, and anyway there were several people approaching, so I waited to see what it meant.

"They came on slowly, stopping to look at everything by the way. At last they got near enough so I could make them out; there were three men and a woman. I recognized one of the men by this time, — our foreman, Sharp. He was guiding the others and I knew then they were visitors, owners probably, because no stranger had ever come before while I was there. The woman, I saw that she was a girl now, called one of the men 'father'; and from the way she spoke I guessed why she was along too. She'd come anyway, whether they approved or not. The drift I was working in was a new one, just opened; and when they got there the whole group stopped a little way off, and Sharp began explaining, talking fast and giving figures. If any of the men saw me they didn't pay any attention; they just listened, and now and then one of them asked a question. But the girl wasn't interested or listening. She was all eyes, looking about here and there, taking in everything; and after a bit she noticed the light in my cap and came peering over to see what it meant. I just stood there watching her and she came quite close, all curiosity, until finally she could see my face. She stopped.

"'Oh,' she said, 'I thought it was just a light. It's a man.'

"'Yes, it's a man,' I said.

"She was looking at me steadily by this time, wholly curious.

"'A—a white man?' she asked.

"I thought a moment, then I understood.

"'Yes, a white man,' I answered.

"She came up to the car at that and looked in. She glanced back at me. Evidently she wasn't entirely satisfied.

"'How old are you?' she asked. 'You look awfully old.'

"I leaned over on the car too; I'd begun to think. I remembered that to me she seemed so very, very young; and all at once it flashed over me that probably I wasn't a day older.

"'Eighteen,' I said.

"'Eighteen!' She stared. 'Why, I'm eighteen. And you—have you been here long?'

"I suppose I smiled. Anyway I know I scared her. She drew back.

"'I don't know,' I said. 'I've forgotten. If you'll tell me the date maybe I can answer. I don't know.'

"'You don't know! You can't mean that.'

"'Yes, I've forgotten.'

"She didn't say a word after that, just looked at me—as a youngster looks when it goes to the circus for the first time. I fancy we stood there half a minute so; then at last, interrupting, the man she'd called 'father' looked over and saw us. He frowned, I could see that, and said something to the foreman. He spoke her name."

Just for a moment Roberts shifted his head, looking at his silent listener steadily. "What do you fancy was that name he called, Elice?"

Elice Gleason started involuntarily, and settled back in her place.

"I haven't the slightest idea, of course."

"It wasn't an ordinary name. At that time I'd never heard it before."

"I'm not good at guessing."

Roberts shifted back to his old position.

"It was 'Elice.' 'Elice, come,' he said.

"The daughter hesitated. I imagine she wanted to ask me several things yet,—whether I had cloven feet, for instance, and lived on spiders; but she didn't. She went back to the other three and they moved on. That was the last I saw of them.

"I worked the rest of that day, did about three men's work, I remember. That night I drew my pay and went to bed; but I didn't go to sleep. I did a lot of thinking and made up my mind to something. I decided I'd been the under dog long enough. I haven't changed the opinion since. Next day I saw the sun when it was straight overhead and soaked the coal dust out of my skin—as much as possible.... That's all of the fourth stage.... Hadn't I better stop?"

The girl shook her head, but still without looking at him.

"No; I want to learn what you did after that, after you woke up."

"I went West. I hadn't seen the sun or the sky for so long that I was hungry for it. In Omaha I fell in with a bunch of cattlemen and, as I always liked to handle stock, that settled it. I accepted an offer as herder; they didn't call it that, but it amounted to the same. I had a half-dozen ponies, rations for six months, and something under a thousand head of stock to look after. By comparison it wasn't work at all; only I was all alone and it took all the time, day and night. I didn't sleep under a roof half a dozen nights from July to October. When the cattle bunched at night I simply rolled up in a blanket where they were and watched the stars until I forgot them; the next thing I knew it was morning. I had hours to read in though, hours and hours; and that was another thing I was after. For I could read, I wasn't quite illiterate, and I was dead in earnest at last. When the Fall round-up came I quit and went to Denver, and portered in a big hotel and went to night school.

"There isn't much to tell after this. I drifted all over the West and the Southwest during the next few years. I got the mining fever and prospected in Colorado and California and Arizona; but I never struck anything. I learned something though; and that was that it isn't the fellow who makes a find who wins, but the chap who buys the prospect, almost invariably. That was useful. Every Winter I landed in a big city and went to school,—night school or mining school or commercial school. Finally it dawned upon me that I was taking the long road to an end, that the short cut was to be really ready to do a thing before making the attempt. I decided to go to a university. That would take years, and meantime I had to live. I could make a living in a little city easier than a big one, so I came here.... You know the rest."

Elice Gleason sat up, her fingers locked over her knees.

"Yes, I know the rest; but—" She was silent.

"But you don't wholly understand," completed the other. "You don't, even yet, do you, Elice?"

"No, not entirely, even yet."

"Why I can't forget when I wish or help being hard?"

"Yes, when you have such infinite possibilities now."

"Now," supplemented the man evenly, "when society at large couldn't pound me down any longer or prevent my getting out of their power."

The girl did not answer.

Deliberately Roberts sat up; no longer listless or tolerantly self-analytic, but very wide awake, very direct.

"I'll have to tell you a few more reasons, then; read between the lines a bit. I never did this before to any one; never will again—to any one. But I must make you understand what made me as I am. I must; you know why. Tell me to stop when you wish, I'll obey gladly; but don't tell me you don't understand.

"To begin again at the beginning. My parents abandoned me. Why? They were starved to it, forced to it. Self-preservation is the first law. I don't clear them, but I understand. They were starving and irresponsible. I merely paid the price of relief, the price society at large demanded.

"At the first home I had afterward the man drank,—drank to forget that he, too, was an under dog. Some one again must pay the price, and I paid it. Now and then I'd succeed in selling a few papers, or do an errand, and earn a few pennies. After the manner of all lesser animals I'd try to hide with them; but he'd find me every time. He seemed to have a genius for it. He'd whip me with whatever was handy; at first for trying to hide, later, when I wouldn't cry, because I was stubborn. Finally, after he'd got tired or satisfied, he'd steal my coppers and head for the nearest bar. Once in January I remember a lady I met on the street took me into a store and bought me a new pair of shoes. I hid them successfully for a week. One day he caught me with them on—and pawned them.

"The old farmer the charity folks traded me to was a Lutheran. Every morning after breakfast he read prayers. He never missed a day. Then he'd send me out with one of his sons,—a grown-up man of twenty-two,—and if I didn't do exactly as much work as the son I went hungry until I got it done if it took half the night. He also had a willow sapling he relied upon when hunger didn't prove effective. He'd pray before he used that too,—pray with one hand gripping my neckband so I couldn't get away. I earned a dollar a day—one single solitary dollar—when I was logging oak in the Ozarks. Day after day when we were on the haul I used to strap myself fast to the load to keep from going to sleep and rolling off under the wheels. I got so dead tired that I fell asleep walking, when I did that to keep awake. You won't believe it, but it's true. I've done it more than once.

"I was sick one day in the coal mine, deathly sick. The air at times was awful. I laid down just outside the car track. I thought I was going to die and felt distinctly pleased at the prospect. Some one reported me to the superintendent. He evidently knew the symptoms, for he came with a pail of water and soaked me where I lay, marked time, and went away. I laid there for three hours in a puddle of water and soft coal grime; then I went back to work. I know it was three hours because my time check was docked exactly that much.

"When I was going to night school in Denver the day clerk, who'd got me the place, took half my tips, the only pay I received, to permit me to hold the place. It was the rule, I discovered, the under-dog penalty.

"I said I never struck anything prospecting. I did. I struck a silver lead down in Arizona. While I was proving it a couple of other prospectors came along, dead broke—and out of provisions. I divided food with them, of course—it's the unwritten law—and they camped for the night. We had supper together. That was the last I knew. When I came to it was thirty-six hours later and I was a hundred miles away in a cheap hotel—without even my bill paid in advance. The record showed that claim was filed on the day I disappeared. The mine is paying a hundred dollars a day now. I never saw those two prospectors again. The present owner bought of them square. I don't hold it up against him.

"I went to night school all one winter in San Francisco with a fellow named Stuart, another under dog like myself. We roomed together in a hall-bedroom to save expense and ate fifteen-cent dinners together at the same soup-house. He clerked in a little tobacco store daytimes. I was running an express elevator. We both saved a little money above what it cost to live. Things went on in this way for four months, until the end of the winter term. One morning when I woke up I found he'd gone. I also found that the little money I'd saved was gone. They went together. I never saw either again.

"I had another friend once, I thought. It was after I'd decided to come here to the university. I was harvesting on a wheat ranch in Nebraska, making money to pay for my matriculation. He was a student too, he said, from New York State, and working for the same purpose. We worked there together all through harvest, boiled side by side in the same sun. One day he announced a telegram from home. His mother was dying. He was crazy almost because he hadn't nearly enough money to take him back at once. And there his mother was in New York State dying! I lent him all I had saved,— seventy odd dollars; and he gave me his note, insisted on doing so— though he hoped the Lord would strike him dead if he failed to return the loan within four days. I have that note yet. Perhaps the Lord did strike him dead. I don't know.

"It was nearly September by this time and harvest was over, my job with it, of course; so I started on east afoot, tramping it. I wasn't a particularly handsome specimen, but still I was clean, and I never asked for a meal without offering to work for it. Yet in the three hundred miles I covered before school opened I had four farmers' wives call the dog,—I recorded the number; and I only slept under a roof two nights.

"Even after I came here, after—Elice, don't! I'm a brute to have done this! From the bottom of my soul I beg your pardon."

The girl was weeping repressedly, her face buried in her hands, her whole body tense.

"Elice, please don't! I'm ashamed. I only wanted you to understand; and now—I'm simply ashamed."

"You needn't be at all." As suddenly as it had come the storm abated, under compulsion. "I wanted to know several things very much; and now I think I do know them. At least I don't wonder any more—why." She stood up decisively, disdaining to dry her eyes.

"But we mustn't stop to chatter any more now," she digressed preventingly. "You made me forget all about time, and cooks should never forget that. It's nearly sundown and father—he'll have been hungry for two hours."

Roberts got to his feet slowly. If in the new light of understanding there was more he had intended saying that day, or if at the sudden barring of opportunity he felt disappointment, his face gave no indication of the fact. He merely smiled in tolerant appreciation of the suggestion last made.

"Doesn't your father know the remedy for hunger yet, at his age?" he queried whimsically.

"Knows it, yes," with an odd laugh; "but it would never occur to him unless some one else suggested it."

A pause, then she looked her companion full in the face, significantly so. "He's dependent and irresponsible as a child or—as Steve Armstrong. They're helpless both, absolutely, left to themselves; and speaking of that, they're both by themselves now." She started for the motor hastily, again significantly so.

"Come, please," she requested.

CHAPTER VI

CRISIS

It was nearly dark when the big red car drew up in front of the Gleason cottage and, the girl only alighting, moved on again slowly down the street. At the second crossing beyond, out of sight of the house, it switched abruptly to the right for four blocks, into the poorer section of the town, and stopped before a battered, old-fashioned residence. A middle-aged man in his shirt sleeves sat on the step smoking a pipe. At a nod from the driver he advanced to the curb.

"Mr. Armstrong in, Edwards?" asked Roberts directly.

The man shook his head.

"Been here, has he?"

"Not since he left this morning; about ten o'clock it was."

Roberts paused, his hand on the clutch lever.

"Will you have him 'phone me when he comes, please?"

"Yes, certainly."

"Thank you."

The next stop was at the office, dark with a Sabbath darkness; but not for long. Within the space of a few minutes after he came, every light switched on, the windows open wide, his coat dangling from a chair in the corner, Roberts was at work upon a small mountain of correspondence collected upon his desk, a mountain of which each unit was marked "personal" or "private." At almost the same time a waiter from a near-by *café* entered with a tray of sandwiches and coffee. Thereafter he ate as he worked.

An hour passed. The sandwiches disappeared entirely and the mountain grew slightly smaller. A second hour dragged by and the mountain suffered a second decline. For the first time Roberts halted and glanced at the clock. A moment later he took down the receiver from the 'phone on his desk and gave a number.

"That you, Randall? Has Armstrong been at your place to-night? You haven't seen him at all to-day, then. No; nothing. Just wanted to know, that was all. Good-night."

Another half-hour passed; then, without pausing in his work, Roberts pulled the buzzer lever for a messenger. When the latter appeared he scribbled a few lines on a sheet of paper, addressed an envelope, and gave it to the boy with half a dollar.

"There's a mate to that coin waiting here for you if you can get me an answer within half an hour," he said. "You know the party, don't you?"

"Sure. Yes, sir."

"Follow up the trail, then. You've lost one minute of your thirty already."

For the third time he returned to his work, halting only when the messenger in blue returned.

"Can't deliver it, sir," explained the latter curtly. "I've been all over town and no one has seen him. Thank you, sir. Good-night."

For several minutes this time Darley Roberts sat in his desk chair thinking, quite motionless. The clock on the wall recorded midnight and he compared the time with his watch to make certain of its accuracy. Once more he took down the telephone receiver.

"This you, Elice?" he asked after a moment. "Can I be of service? Never mind, no need to explain. I understand. I'll be right up."

In spite of the city speed limit the big red car made those twelve blocks intervening in sixty-four seconds flat.

"How did you ever know?" —infinite wonder, infinite relief as well in the tone. "Tell me that, please."

"I didn't know, of course. I merely guessed. Has it been long?"

Involuntarily the girl shuddered, then held herself steady with an effort.

"Yes, since dinner. He came while we were eating; and father—"

"I understand," preventingly. "Don't worry. It's all over with now. Did any one else see—any of the neighbors, I mean?"

"I think not. It was after dark and—Oh, it's simply horrible! horrible!"

"Yes," gently. "I appreciate that. Let's not speak about it. Your two roomers are both in?"

The girl nodded.

"They didn't suspect anything wrong either?"

"No, the hammock was dark—and father watched. They went right up to their rooms without stopping."

Roberts nodded, and looked out of the window. The light in the residence district of the town was on a midnight schedule and was now cut off. He turned back. A moment he stood so, silent, facing the girl there in the dimly lighted hall. Under a sudden instinct he reached out and laid a hand compellingly on each of her shoulders, holding her captive.

"You don't misunderstand my intruding here to-night, do you, Elice?" he asked directly.

"Misunderstand!" The girl looked at him steadily, the dark circles about her eyes eloquent. "Never. How can you fancy such a thing! Never."

"And you're willing to trust me to bring everything out right? It will be all right, take my word for that."

Still the girl did not stir, but gazed at him. "Yes, I trust you implicitly, always," she said.

A moment longer the hands held their place before they dropped.

"All right, then," he said perfunctorily, "go to bed. I'll take care of Steve—to-night and in the future. Don't worry. Good-night."

"Wait," a hand was upon his arm, a compelling hand. "You mean—"

Roberts smiled deliberately, his slow, impersonal smile.

"Exactly what I said. This will be a lesson Steve should never forget. I can't imagine his repeating it—ever. Besides, I'll help him not to. I have a plan."

"You mean to help him as—as you helped Harry Randall and Margery?"

A moment the man was silent, though he smiled.

"No, not exactly. I'll merely assist him to help himself. I think perhaps it's only my duty anyway, that maybe I'm more or less responsible. By the way, don't be surprised if he disappears for a bit. He may possibly decide to go out of town. That's all, for now."

The girl drew a long breath.

"You responsible!" she echoed. "If you're responsible, how, then, about—myself?"

"Elice!" Roberts cut her off peremptorily. "I refuse to listen. Go to bed at once, I insist. I'll come to-morrow and talk if you wish. Just now it's all too near. Good-night again."

An instant later, on the darkened porch without, he had the arm of the doddering old man in the grip of a vise.

"Leave everything here to me," he said swiftly, "and see to Elice." He was leading the other toward the entrance. "Listen. See that she goes to bed—at once; and you too. I'll attend to everything else. Trust me," and very gently he himself closed the door behind the other two.

It was after office hours of the day following when Stephen Armstrong, a bit pale but carefully groomed this time, entered the outer room of Darley Roberts' office and, with decided reluctance, approached the private apartment beyond. The door was open. Seated before the big desk, shirt-sleeved as usual, Roberts sat working. As the newcomer approached he wheeled about.

"Come in," he said simply. "I'm glad to see you."

The visitor took a seat by the open window and looked out rather obviously.

"I just received your note a bit ago," he began perfunctorily, "and called instead of giving you an appointment, as you asked. It's the least I could do after last night." He halted, looking at the building opposite steadily. "I want you to know that I appreciate thoroughly what you did for me then. I—I'm heartily ashamed, of course."

"Don't speak of it, please," swiftly. "I've forgotten it and I'm sure Miss Gleason and her father have done the same. No one else knows, so let's consider it never occurred. It never will again, I'm sure, so what's the use of remembering? Is it agreed?"

Armstrong's narrow shoulders lifted in silence.

"As for not speaking of it again," he answered after a moment, "yes. Whether or not in the future, however—I'm not liar enough to promise things I can't deliver."

"But you can 'deliver,' as you say," shortly. "You know it yourself."

Armstrong shook his head.

"I'm not as bumptious as I was a few years ago," he commented. "I'd have said 'yes' then undoubtedly. Now—I don't know."

Roberts swung about in his desk chair, the crease between his eyes suddenly grown deep.

"Nonsense," he refuted curtly. "You're not the first man in the world who has done something to regret. Every one has in some way or another—and profited by the experience. It's forgotten already, I say, man. Let it pass at that, and go ahead as though nothing had happened. By the way, have you had supper—or do you call it dinner?"

For the first time Armstrong looked at the speaker and, forgetting for the instant, he almost smiled. The question was characteristic.

"I've already dined, thank you," he said.

Without comment Roberts called up the *café* and ordered delivered his customary busy-day lunch of sandwiches and coffee.

"I'm going East on the eleven-fifty limited to-night," he explained, "and there are several things I've got to see to first." In voluntary relaxation from work he slipped down in the big chair until his head rested on the back. Thereafter for a long time, for longer doubtless than he realized, he sat so, looking at the other man; not rudely or unpleasantly, but with the old, absent, analytical expression large upon his face. At last he roused.

"I suppose," he began abruptly, "you're wondering what it is I wish to speak with you about. I'll explain in advance that it's of your personal affairs purely, nothing else. Would you prefer me not to intrude?"

For a moment Armstrong did not answer, but with an effort he looked at the questioner directly.

"If it were a couple of days back," he said, "I should have answered 'yes' emphatically. Now—" his glance wandered out the window, resting on the brick wall opposite, "now I hardly know. You've earned a sort of right to wield the probe; and besides—"

"Never mind the right," shortly. "I tell you last night is forgotten. I meant to see you and have the same talk anyway—with your permission."

Still Armstrong hesitated, looking steadily away. "You've condoned the fact, then, that I've cut you dead on the street regularly?"

"I understood—and didn't blame you. There are dozens of people who know Old Man Roberts and still never see him when passing face to face. It's all in the game."

At last Armstrong's glance returned, almost with wonder. "And you don't lay it up against them?"

"Sometimes. Usually, however, not. Life's too short to play with toys; and enmities are toys—double-edged ones at that. You haven't answered my question yet."

"I know; but just a moment more. Do you recall, by the way, a prophecy I made once, years ago?"

"Yes; it never came true as far as I am concerned."

"Perhaps you never had cause to have it do so."

"Possibly."

"With me it did come about. I've hated you ever since—from the day you left. Do you realize why I haven't answered your question?"

"Yes, why you haven't. I'm still waiting."

"I'm wondering," mused Armstrong, "why I don't hate you, now that we're here together. I've thought a lot of bitter things about you, more than about any one in the world. I don't know why I don't say them now that I've got the chance."

"Yes, you have the chance. I'm listening."

"I know." Armstrong's long fingers were twitching nervously. Despite an effort to prevent his lower lip trembled in sympathy. "And still, now that for the first time I have the chance, I can't. I don't want to. I—" Of a sudden an uncontrollable moisture came into his eyes, and he shifted about abruptly until his face was hid. "Damn you, Darley Roberts!" he stormed inadequately, "I don't want to a bit, but after all I trust you and—and like you. You have my permission to intrude. I want you to, have wanted you to a hundred times." The Rubicon was crossed at last and he made the admission that for long had trembled on his tongue. "Somehow I can't get along without you and keep my nerve. I think you're the only person in the world who even in a measure understands me, and can maybe make a man of me again."

"You mean to suggest that Elice," he began, "that Elice—You dare to suggest that to me?"

In his place Darley Roberts sat looking at the other, merely looking at him. The silence grew embarrassing, lasted into minutes; but still unconsciously he remained as he was. At last suddenly his eyes dropped and simultaneously the fingers of his big hands twitched in a way that heralded action. Whatever the problem of that period of silence decision had come.

"I think I understand what you mean," he said deliberately. "Perhaps, too, it's true. I don't know. Anyway I'll try to play the game—try to." He remembered, and the hands lay still. "By the way, you're not working now?"

"No."

"Have you anything definite in sight?"

Despite the permission he had granted but a moment before Armstrong colored; with an effort he met his questioner frankly.

"No," again.

"That's good. It occurred to me that it might clear the atmosphere here a bit if you went away for a time. What do you say to McLean's for a couple of weeks?"

On Armstrong's face the red of a moment ago changed to white, a white which spread to his very lips.

"And take the cure, you mean! Do you think, really, it's as bad with me as that?"

"No," bluntly; "I'd have said so if I had. But just because you might not contract pneumonia is no reason for not wearing an overcoat when the thermometer is at zero. I'd go if I were you, just as I'd be vaccinated if there was an epidemic of small-pox prevalent."

"But the admission! A confirmed alcoholic!"

"Confirmed nothing. Your going is no one's business but your own. The place is a general sanatorium; it's advertised so. Anyway you will have good company. The biggest bondholder in the Traction Company is there now. Do you happen to have the money that you'll need convenient?"

"No. That's another rub; and besides—on the square, Darley, I don't need to do that—yet. I know after last night things look bad; but—"

"I understand perfectly. Let's not waste ammunition on a man of straw. The change will do you good, though, anyway. I'd go myself for the sake of that big marble plunge if I could spare the time." He was writing a check swiftly. "Pay it back when something drops," he proffered; "there will be something develop soon—there always is. By the way, why not go along with me to-night? It's on the same road."

Armstrong accepted the slip of paper mechanically; a real moisture came into his eyes, and he held it back at arm's length.

"Darley, confound you," he protested, "I can't accept that. I simply can't!"

"Can't—why? It's good. Try it anywhere down town."

"You know I don't mean that; but—"

"Yes—" The big fingers were twitching ominously.

"But after—what's past—"

"Wouldn't you make me a loan if positions were reversed?" shortly.

"Yes, certainly; but—"

"Forget it, then." Roberts turned back to his desk abruptly. "Pardon me if I go on working. I've simply got to clear this desk before I go." He waited in silence until the other man started to leave; just as Armstrong reached the door he wheeled about.

"You'll be with me at eleven-fifty sure, won't you?" he asked directly.

Armstrong hesitated, his eyes averted.

"Yes," he said at last.

"Good. I'll attend to the reservations for both of us. Travel East is light now and we'll have things practically to ourselves. There are a number of other things I wish to talk with you about—and we'll have all night to do it in. I suppose you'll see Elice this evening?"

Again Armstrong colored. "Yes," he repeated uncertainly.

"Tell her, please, for me that I'll be out of town for about three weeks. Meanwhile the car is subject to her order. I left directions at the garage. If it's convenient for you to happen around this way about train time there'll be a cab waiting. Good-bye until then."

For two hours thereafter Roberts worked steadily—until every scrap of correspondence on the desk had been answered or bore memoranda for the instruction of the stenographer on the morrow. At last he took down the 'phone.

"Randall? There'll be a carriage call for my baggage shortly. It's all ready. Thanks. By the way, have you that manuscript handy I spoke to you once about? All right. Tuck it in somewhere while you think of it, please. You're still of the same opinion, that it's good; at least worth a hearing? Very well. It'll be published then. I'm accepting your judgment. Never mind how. This is between you and me absolutely. I'm not to figure—ever. If it goes flat he'll have had his chance. That's all any of us can have. By the way, again. I'm sorry to miss Mrs. Randall's dinner-party. I'm not often honored in that way. Anyway, though, perhaps it's as well. I'm impossible socially; and, fortunately, I know just enough to realize it. Yes; that's all. Good-night."

Thereafter he waited until he got "Central" on the wire.

"Call me at eleven-thirty," he requested. "I'll be asleep, so ring me long and loud. Eleven-thirty sharp, remember, please."

He hung up the instrument with a gesture of relief and leaned back in his chair, his great bushy head against the bare oak, his big hands loose in his lap. A half-minute perhaps he sat so—until the eyes slowly closed and, true to his word, and swiftly as a child at close of day, he fell asleep.

At eleven o'clock the watchman of the building, noticing the light, came to investigate. A moment he stood in the open door, an appreciative observer. On tiptoe he moved away.

"Some one's paying good and plenty for this," he commented *sotto voce* and with a knowing wag of the head. "The old man's all in— and he isn't doing it for his health alone, you bet!"

CHAPTER VII

TRAVESTY

Out in the street, in front of the Gleason cottage, the red car glistened in the moonlight. In the shade of the familiar veranda Roberts tossed his gauntlets and cap on the floor and drew forth two wicker rocking-chairs where they would catch the slight midsummer night wind.

"Hottest night of the season, I fancy," he commented, as he helped his companion remove her dust coat and waited thereafter until she was seated before he took the place by her side. "Old Reliable number two certainly did us a good turn this evening. Runs like an advertisement, doesn't it?"

It was a minute before the girl answered. "Yes. It sounds cheap to say so, but at times, like to-night, it almost seems to me Paradise. It makes one forget, temporarily, the things one wishes to forget."

"Yes," said her companion.

"I suppose people who have been accustomed to luxuries all their lives don't think of it at all; but others—" She was silent.

"Yes," said Roberts again, "I think I understand. It's the one compensation for being hungry a long time, I suppose; the added enjoyment of the delayed meal when at last it is served. At least that's what those who never went hungry say. I hope you'll get a lot of pleasure out of the machine this Summer."

The girl looked at him quickly.

"I? Are you going away again?"

"Yes. I start West to-morrow. Things are moving faster than I expected."

"And you won't take the car with you?"

"No, I shan't play again for a time. I always had a theory that a man should know a business he conducts, not take some one else's word for it. I'm going to put on my corduroys and live with that mine until it grows up. I don't even know how long that will be. In a way to-night is good-bye."

The girl said nothing this time.

"I meant what I said, though, in regard to the car," returned Roberts. "I shall be disappointed if you don't use it a lot. I've always felt as though it sort of belonged to us together, we've had such a lot of pleasure out of it in common. They tell me at the garage that while I was away last time it wasn't out at all. Didn't Steve deliver my message?"

"Yes."

"Won't you promise to do differently the rest of the season?"

Again the girl paused before she answered.

"No," she said then. "You understand why?"

"Not if I request otherwise?"

"Don't request it, please," swiftly, "as a favor. I repeat, you understand."

"Understand, certainly, what you mean to imply." The big hands on the man's knees drooped a little wearily. "You don't trust me wholly, even yet, do you, Elice?" he added abruptly.

"Trust you! That's a bit cruel."

The man shifted in his seat unconsciously.

"If it was I beg your pardon," he said gently. "I didn't intend it so. I suppose I'm wrong; but what others, mere observers, say seems to me so trivial. The gossip of people who'd knife you without compunction the instant your back was turned for their own gratification or gain—to let them judge and sentence—pardon me once more. I shan't mention the matter again."

The girl looked steadily out into the night, almost as though its peace were hers. "Yes," she returned, "you are wrong—but in a different way than you intimated. It isn't what others would say at all that prevents my accepting, but my own judgment of myself. You've done so many things for me; and I in return—I'm never able to do anything whatever. It's a matter of self-respect wholly. One can't accept, and accept, and accept always—in the certainty of remaining permanently in debt."

The man looked at her oddly. Then he glanced away.

"No; I suppose not," he acquiesced.

"If there were anything I could do for you in turn to make up even partially; but you're so big and independent and self-sufficient—"

"Self-sufficient!" Roberts caught the dominant word and dwelt on it meditatively. "I suppose I am that way. It never occurred to me before." The big hands tightened suddenly, their weariness gone. "But let's forget it," he digressed energetically. "This is the last time I'll see you for a long time, months at least; and a lot can happen in months sometimes. The future is the Lord's, but the present is ours. Let's enjoy it while we may. What, by the way, are you going to do the remainder of the Summer?"

"Do?" The girl laughed shortly. "What I'm doing now, I fancy, mostly. Father will be away the first week in September. I promised Margery I'd stay with her during that time; otherwise—" A gesture completed the sentence.

Roberts looked at her oddly. "Is that what you want to do—you?" he asked bluntly.

"Want to do?" Again the laugh. "What does it matter what I want to do?" She caught herself suddenly. "Margery and I may go away to a lake somewhere during that week," she completed.

"And after that?" suggested the man.

"The university will be open then. I've secured a place this year,— assistant in English."

"You're really serious, Elice?" soberly. "This is news to me, you know. You really purpose teaching in future?"

"Yes." She returned her companion's look steadily. "Father was not reappointed for the coming session. He's over the age line. I supposed you knew."

"No; I didn't know before." Without apparent reason Roberts stood up. The great hands were working again. A moment he stood there so, the big bushy head outlined distinctly against the starlit sky; with equal abruptness he returned to his seat.

"What a farce this is you and I are playing," he said. "Do you really wish it to go on longer?"

The girl did not look at him, did not move.

"Farce?" she echoed.

The man gestured swiftly.

"Don't do that, please," he prevented. "You and I know each other entirely too well to pretend. I repeat, do you wish this travesty to go on indefinitely? If you do I accept, of course—but—do you?"

Instinctively, as on a former occasion, the girl drew her chair farther back on the porch, until her face was in the shadow. It was out of the shadow that she spoke.

"Prefer it to go on? Yes," she said; "because I wish you to remain as you are now. But really wish it, no; because it's unfair, wholly unfair."

"Unfair to me?"

"Yes, to you."

For the second time Roberts gestured. "Take that consideration out of the discussion absolutely, please," he said. "With that understanding do you still wish this pretence to go on?"

"I wish to keep your friendship."

"My friendship—nothing more? I'm brutally blunt, I realize; but I can't let to-night, this last night, go by without knowing something of how you feel. You never have given me even so much as a hint, you know. I've waited patiently, I think, for you to select the moment for confidence; but you avoid it always; and to-morrow at this time—You know I love you, Elice. Knowing that, do you still wish me to go away pretending merely polite friendship? Do you wish it to be that way, Elice?"

The girl ignored the question, ignored all except the dominant statement.

"Yes, I know you love me," she echoed. "You told me so once before."

"Once! A thousand times; you understood the language. It seems foolish even to reiterate the fact now. And yet you've never answered."

"I know. I said it was unfair; and still—"

"You won't answer even yet."

"I can't. I'm drifting and waiting for light. Don't misunderstand; that isn't religion—I've not been to church in a year, or said a prayer. It isn't that at all. I simply don't want to hate myself, or be hated by another justly later."

"And you expect to drift on until that light comes?"

A halt, long enough for second thought or renewal of a decision. "I can't do otherwise. There's no other way. It's inevitable."

"'Inevitable!'" Roberts shrugged impatiently. "I don't like the word. It belongs in the same class with 'chance' and 'predestination' and 'luck.' There are few things inevitable except death."

"This is one—that I must wait."

"And you can't even take me into your confidence, about the reason why? Mind, I don't ask it unless you voluntarily desire. I merely suggest."

"No," steadily; "I can't tell you the reason. I've got to decide for myself—when light comes."

Roberts' great shoulders squared significantly.

"But if I know it already," he suggested evenly, "what then?"

No answer, although the other waited half a minute.

"I repeat: what if I know it already?"

"Do you know?"

Roberts' glance wandered into the shadow where the girl was, then returned slowly to the street and the red car.

"I rode East with Steve Armstrong," he said, "as far as he went. I also wired him when I was coming, and we returned together. He told me, I think, everything—except about your father. He forgot that, if he knew. Do you doubt I know the reason, Elice?"

Out of the shadow came the girl's face,—the face only.

"You did this for Stephen Armstrong—after what is past! Why?"

"Because life is short and I wanted to know several things before I came to-night. Would you like to hear what it was I wished to learn?"

Again the face vanished.

"Yes," said a voice.

"You know already, so it won't be news. One was that he still cares for you—as always. He perjured himself once, because he thought it was his duty; but he has never ceased to care. The other thing was that he's changed his mind and is going back to his literary work. His novel, that was accepted tentatively, will be published next Winter. What else I learned is immaterial. I don't often venture a prediction, but in his case I'll make the exception. I believe that this time he'll make good. He has the incentive—and experience. Do you still doubt I know the reason, Elice?"

"No. But that you should tell me this!"

"I claim no virtue. You knew it already. I'm merely attempting to simplify—to aid the coming of the light."

For the second time out of the shadow came the girl's face, her whole figure. "Darley Roberts," asked a voice, "are you human, or aren't you? I don't believe another man in the world would, under like circumstances, do as you have done by Steve Armstrong. I can't believe you human merely."

The man smiled oddly; the look passed.

"I have merely played the game fair," he explained dispassionately, "or tried to, according to my standard. Like yourself, I don't want to hate myself in the future, whatever comes. The hate of others—I'm indifferent to that, Elice."

"And still you love me."

"I shall never care for another, never. The time when I could, if it ever existed, is past."

The white hands dropped helplessly into the girl's lap.

"I thought I understood you," she said, "and yet, after all—"

"We live but once," gently. "I wish you to be happy, the happiest possible. Does that help?"

"Yes, but—" In a panic the face, the hands, retreated back into the shadow again. "Oh, I'm afraid of you once more, afraid of you," she completed.

A moment the man sat still; then came his unexpected deliberate smile.

"No; not afraid. I repeat you know me absolutely, and we're never afraid of things we know. I explained once before that that's why I went through the detail of telling you everything. You're not afraid of me in the least, any more than I am afraid of you."

"No?"

The smile still held.

"No."

"And still—"

"I repeat, it isn't fear of me that prevents your answering." Like a flash the smile vanished. Simultaneously the voice dropped until it was very low, yet very steady. "You love me in return, Elice, girl. It isn't that!"

From the darkness silence, just silence.

"I say, you love me in return. Can you deny it?"

Still not an answering sound nor a motion.

Roberts drew a long breath. His big eloquent hands hung free. "Shall I put in words the exact reason you won't answer, to prove I know?" he asked.

"Yes." The voice was just audible.

A moment Roberts paused. "It's because you are afraid, not of me, but of Steve Armstrong: afraid of the way the Lord fashioned him. Elice, come out into the light, please. We must face this thing. You're not his mother, and you don't love him otherwise. Tell me, is a sentiment dead greater than one living? Will you, must you, sacrifice the happiness of two for the happiness of one? Answer me, please."

An instant the girl hesitated; obediently she came out into the light, stood there so, her hand on the pillar of the porch. She did not glance at her companion, did not dare to do so.

"I repeat, I can't answer you yet," she said simply. "It's bitter, cruel to you, I know, and to myself; but it would be infinitely worse if—if I made a mistake." She paused, while a restless hand swept across her face. "I can't help feeling that I'm to blame a good deal already, that if I hadn't changed, and shown the change—" She sat down helplessly, the sentence incomplete. "Oh, I can't bear to think of it. It drives me mad. To feel you have the responsibility of another's very soul on your hands, and to have failed in that trust—"

"Elice!"

"Don't stop me. It's true. If I had married him years ago when he first wished me to do so he'd never have gone down. I cared for him then, or fancied I did so; and I could have held him up. But instead—"

"Elice! I won't listen. You're morbid and see ghosts where nothing exists. You're no more to blame for being human and awakening than lightning is to blame when it strikes." He stood up, suddenly. "Besides, the past is dead. To attempt to revive it is useless. The future alone matters; and it's that I wish to talk about. I can't bear to think of going away and leaving you as you are now. It's preposterous. If you cared for Steve I shouldn't insist for a moment, or trouble you again so long as I lived; but you don't care for him." He took a step forward, and stopped where she must look him in the face. "You don't care for him, that way, do you, Elice?" he asked.

Straight in the eyes the girl answered his look. But the lips spoke nothing.

"And you do love me, love me, don't you, girl?"

Still not a word; only that same steady look.

"Elice,"—the man's hands were on her shoulders, holding her immovable,—"answer me. This is unbearable. Don't you love me? Say it. I must know."

Bit by bit the long lashes dropped, until the dark eyes were hid. "I can't say it yet," she said, "you know that. Don't compel me to."

"Cannot or will not?"

Still no answer, merely silence.

Just noticeably the man's big hands tightened their grip. "I can make you very happy, Elice, girl," he voiced swiftly; "I know it; because I have the ability and I love you. I'll take you away, to any place in the world you wish to go, stay as long as you wish, do whatever you choose. I'll give you anything you want, anything you ever wanted. I have the power to do this now, and I'll have more power in future. Nothing can stop me now or prevent, except death alone. Say the word and I'll not go West to-morrow. Instead, we'll begin to live. We're both starved for the good things that life has to offer. We'll eat our fill together, if you but say the word. We've wasted years—both of us, long, precious years. There's a big, big debt owing us; but at last, at last—"

"Darley Roberts!"

The man suddenly halted, passive.

"You don't realize what you're doing, what you're saying. It's unworthy of you."

A moment longer the grip of the big hands still clung as it was. They dropped, and the man drew back.

"Unworthy?" He looked at her steadily. "Can you fancy I was trying to—buy you? I thought you realized I love you."

"I do. But—you're only making it harder for me—to do right."

"Do right?" Once more the echo. "Right!" He laughed, as his companion had never before heard him laugh. "I wonder if it is right to make a certain cripple of one human being on the chance of making a real weakling less weak? Right to—" a sudden tense halt. "I beg your pardon," swiftly. "I didn't mean that. Forget that I said it." He stooped to pick up his cap and gauntlets. When he came forward once more he was himself again, as he would be from that moment on.

"Don't fancy for a minute I mean to hurt you, or to make it harder for you now," he said steadily; "but this is the end, you realize, the turning of the ways—and I must be sure. You still can't give me an answer, Elice?"

The girl did not look at him this time, did not stir.

"No, not even yet."

A pause, short this time.

"And you won't reconsider about going to work for a living, won't let me help, as a friend, merely as a friend? You know me too well to misunderstand this. It would mean nothing absolutely to me now to help, and would not alter our friendship, if you wish, in the least. Won't you let me do this trifle for you if I ask it?"

Resolutely the girl shook her head, very steadily.

"I understand and appreciate," she said; "but I can't."

A moment longer the man waited. He extended his hand. "There's nothing more to be said, then, I fancy, except good-bye."

For the first time in that long, long fight the girl weakened. Gropingly she found the extended hand; but even then the voice was steady.

"Good-bye," she said—and that was all.

CHAPTER VIII

CELEBRATION

It had been a gay dinner, a memorable dinner. The mere ostensible occasion of its being in celebration of the publication of Steve Armstrong's first novel, "The Disillusioned," would of itself have been sufficient reason therefor. In addition, the resignation, by a peculiar coincidence to take effect the same day, of the former manager of the Traction Company, Darley Roberts, with a recommendation that was virtually a command for the advancement of his acting assistant, Harry Randall, to his place, added another reason no less patent. If a cloud existed that evening to mar the happiness of those four long-time friends gathered in commemoration of the dispensation of Providence jointly enjoyed, it most emphatically had not lifted its head above the surface. Never had Margery Randall bubbled with more spontaneous abandon; or, even in the old university days, had Elice Gleason laughed more easily. And as for Steve Armstrong, the guest of honor, the conquering hero,—it was his hour and in its intoxicating completeness he had enjoyed it to the full; had stretched it on and on that he might enjoy it again. Now, the last course served, the last toast proposed and drunk in inadequate chocolate, and the two girl friends, after the habit of old acquaintances, left to their own private confab, Randall and Armstrong drifted instinctively upstairs to the former's den for their after-dinner smoke. In absolute well-being, too keen almost for words, Armstrong dropped into a big leather chair, facing his host.

"By Jove, Harry," he commented explosively, "I tell you this is something like living. I never enjoyed myself so much before in my life."

Harry Randall, decidedly stouter than the Randall of professor days, smiled appreciatively as he selected a cigar from the convenient humidor.

"Yes, the world does look rather bright to me to-night, I'll admit," he acquiesced.

"Bright!" Armstrong laughed outright in pure animal exuberance. "It's positively dazzling: the more so by comparison." He looked at his companion with the frank understanding of those long and intimately acquainted. "What a change a few short years can make sometimes, can't they? What an incredible change!"

Harry Randall returned the look, but gravely this time.

"Yes, I've been thinking of that all the evening," he said simply.

"So have I." Armstrong laughed shortly; "that is, when I haven't been too irresponsibly happy to think at all. Just to get my bearings I tried to fancy myself back where I was once when I came to tell my troubles to you; and went to pieces at the end of the narrative." He gestured eloquently. "What a fool I was and what a liar to swear I'd never do any more literary work, or permit a book of mine to be published in any circumstances, ever!" Once more the gesture, ending in an all-comprehensive shrug. "Bah! I don't like to think of it. The whole thing's a nightmare, neither more nor less!"

Again Harry Randall did not smile.

"Yes; the past was a little that way," he echoed again.

For perhaps half a minute Armstrong smoked in reminiscent gravity; swiftly as the shadow had intruded it passed.

"Let's forget it," he proposed, "forget it absolutely and never speak of it again. By the way, do you own this place now?"

"No; Roberts still holds it. I made him an offer before he went away last Summer, but he wouldn't even consider it then. I'll try again when he returns. Margery wants it badly."

"When he returns? Is he coming back soon?"

"I judge so, although I've had no word. There were a number of letters and telegrams came for him yesterday, and a batch of them to-day. I suspect that he intended being here to-night and is delayed for some reason." Randall removed his glasses and polished them with unnecessary diligence. "I wired him when I heard what he'd done for me, but I haven't had any answer yet. I'd have given anything to have had him here to-night. It was the one thing lacking."

For a moment there was silence.

"He has done a lot for you, Harry, that's a fact," commented Armstrong, judicially. "Your new place at six thousand dollars a year is a pretty good thing even for these days."

"A lot? Everything! He pulled me out of hell and gave me a chance when I'd never have made one myself. I owe him everything; and I've never been able to do him one blessed service in return."

Armstrong squirmed uncomfortably. The usually reticent Harry Randall like this was a novelty.

"For that matter, he's done a lot for both of us," admitted Armstrong, perfunctorily. "I appreciate it too, thoroughly."

Randall looked up swiftly; in remembrance equally swift he turned away.

"Yes; he's done miracles for both of us, more than we can possibly realize," he said softly. "More—"

"Harry," interrupted Margery Randall's voice from the stairway, "I'm sorry to hasten you men, but Elice thinks she must go. Her father isn't well, you know, and is at home alone."

"I'll wait, Elice. It's early yet. See how your father is and come down when you can." Armstrong looked at her meaningly, with all but an appeal. "This is my night, you know. You really can't refuse to let me see you to-night."

The girl busied herself with the lights and the gas in the grate.

"I know, Steve; but really I'd rather not see any one longer to-night." She took off her coat almost hurriedly. "It's a busy time for me now before the holidays; and with father as he is—That's why I came away so early, you know. Not to-night, please, Steve."

Armstrong silently paced the length of the little library, pitifully bare in comparison with the home they had just left. He halted.

"Do you realize that you've invariably prevented, by one excuse or another, my talking with you alone in months now?" he asked abruptly. "Don't you mean ever to give me a chance again? You know what it is I wish to speak about, Elice."

The girl was standing—quite still now.

"Yes, I know what it is you wish," she corroborated.

Armstrong fingered the gloves in his hand nervously. "Aren't you going to listen then? I won't attempt to make any apologies for the past. I can't. But I'd hoped you'd forgotten, or at least forgiven, by this time. I've tried to make good, honestly, Elice; and to-night particularly—don't stand me in the corner any longer, please. I've been punished enough."

"Punished!" The girl wheeled. "I wonder—" She checked herself suddenly. "Very well," she digressed swiftly,—"wait. I'll be back soon," and she was gone.

Alone Armstrong threw hat and topcoat into a chair almost irritably; walking over to the grate, he stood gazing down into the blaze absently. For some reason it called to mind another grate and another occasion when he had looked absently therein; and almost unconsciously he caught himself glancing at the shelf above, half expecting to catch the play of light from a red decanter thereon. With the shrug of one who banishes an unpleasant memory he turned away. He was still standing, however, when the girl returned.

"Is there any way I can assist, with your father?" he asked perfunctorily.

"No, thank you. He's asleep. It's mental, the trouble with him, more than anything else." She sat down and indicated a place opposite. "I'm so glad Harry Randall escaped in time."

"And I as well?"

"Yes, and you, assuredly."

Armstrong waited; but she said no more, and with an odd diffidence he cleared his throat unnecessarily.

"It's sacrilege, though, for us to talk commonplaces to-night," he anticipated hastily. "There's too much else to discuss, and to-day has meant too much. Do you realize what this day really means for both of us, Elice?"

The long fingers lay in the girl's lap, quite still.

"Perhaps. But tell me if you wish."

Again the fantastic diffidence held Armstrong in its grip; and again he freed himself with an effort.

"It means, first of all, that at last I'm on my feet, where I've always wished to be. It means that I'm to have my chance—and that again means independence." He overlooked absolutely the egotism of the statement, was unconscious of it. Success loomed too big and incontestible; possible future failure lay too remote to merit consideration. "It means all of this; but beyond that it means that I have the right to tell you again that I love you. You know I love you, as always, Elice."

"As always?"

"Forget, please. This is to-day; my day, our day. You don't doubt I love you?"

"No; I don't doubt it."

Armstrong breathed deep. An instinct all but overwhelming impelled him to rise, to—he substituted with his eyes.

"You realize all that I wish to say," he said swiftly, "so why make a farce of it by words? We've drifted apart for a long time, a hideously long time, and it's been my fault throughout; but now that it's over won't you come back to the beginning, Elice, to the place where we separated?" He halted for breath, for words where none were adequate. "I want you, Elice, want you—now and always. Tell me, please, that you've forgiven me, that you'll come back."

In the girl's lap the hands crossed steadily; again that was the only move she made.

"So far as I am concerned there's nothing to forgive, nor has there ever been," she said gently. "As for going back, though, I can't; because I can't. It's useless to lie, for you'd find me out. I've simply awakened."

"You mean you—don't care for me any more?"

"No; I care for you very much; but not in that way. It was so before the end came. I awoke before that."

"And still you would have married me then."

"Yes," simply.

"And now?"

The girl did not answer, did not even look up.

"And now," he repeated insistently, "tell me; and now?"

This time the brown eyes lifted, met his steadily.

"Unless something happens I can't marry you now," she said.

Armstrong looked at her; at first dazedly, then with a trace of color gathering under his fair skin.

"Unless something happens?" he repeated. "Pardon me, but what do you mean by that?"

"Nothing," swiftly. "I was thinking of something else. I hate to hurt you; but as I said before, it's useless to temporize. I can't marry you now, Steve."

In his place Armstrong settled back dumbly. Unconsciously he passed his handkerchief over his mouth. The hand that carried it trembled a bit.

"You really mean that, do you?" he groped, half to himself, "mean the break to be really final this time?" He shut his eyes, like a child suddenly awakened in the dark and afraid. "Somehow I hadn't expected that at all, hadn't planned on it. I suppose it was childish of me; but I've been taking things for granted, on the strength of the past, and—and—" Of a sudden the rambling tongue halted. The eyes opened wide, unnaturally wide; and in their depths was again that new look of terror, but now magnified. "Tell me that you don't mean it, Elice, really," he pleaded. "I was just beginning to live and hope again; and now—tell me!"

Long before this the girl had ceased looking at him. Instead, with the instinctive fascination an open fire exerts over all human beings, she had turned toward the tiny jets of gas in the grate; her face propped in her hands she sat staring into the depths of the flame. She scarcely seemed to breathe, even when she spoke.

"Yes, I meant it," she repeated patiently.

For a long time there was silence,—long enough with the man for the mood to pass, the mood of terror, and in reaction its antithesis, reckless abandon, to come in its stead. For come it did, as was inevitable; and heralding its approach sounded a laugh,—a sudden mirthless, sarcastic laugh.

"So this is the end of my day," he said. He laughed again. "I might have known it was too good to last. What a fool I was to imagine that just because one thing had come my way everything else was going to follow suit. What a poor, blithering fool!"

"Steve!" No lethargy in the girl's figure now, in the face of a sudden turned toward him appealingly. "Don't take it that way or say such things. Nothing has changed in the least. I'm still your friend, as I've always been; so is Harry Randall—and the rest. You're still a successful writer; you've proved it to-day, and you'll prove it further with the new book you're working on now. I repeat, nothing has altered in the least. Don't talk that way. It hurts me."

In his chair, erect now, Armstrong merely smiled. But his color was higher than normal and the blue eyes were unnaturally bright.

"No, nothing has changed, I suppose," he said evenly. "You're right there. I've simply been in a trance—that's all—and I've inadvertently come to. I seem to have the habit of doing that." He smiled again, hopelessly cruel in his egotism. "Of course I have friendship, oceans of it, yours particularly, as I've had all the time. And success; it monopolizes the sky, fairly blots out the stars, and obscures the sun like an eclipse. There's no end to the success I have. It's infinite. And still further, incentive: to be and to do and to fight." The smile vanished. He could not mock in the face of that thought even yet. "Incentive! What a travesty. Elice, you've killed the last trace of incentive I had just now."

"Steve!" The girl's hands lifted imperiously. "Stop. Have you no pity?" She shook the swift-gathering flood from her eyes rebelliously and faced him fair. "You'll be very sorry you said such things after you've had time to think," she went on. "Don't add regret to the rest to-night. Please don't."

"Sorry, perhaps," echoed the man, "and regret—possibly. Anyway, what does it matter? It's true."

"True—no," swiftly. "I can't believe it. I won't. Don't say that. In pity, don't."

"But, I repeat, it is true," doggedly. "I at least can't help that. Elice, don't cry so!" Of a sudden he was on his feet bending over her. "Please don't. I love you!"

"Don't touch me! I can't stand it!" The girl had drawn away swiftly, the repression of years for an instant broken. "You dare to tell me that—now! Love—" She cut herself short with an effort of will and, rising hurriedly, walked the length of the room to the window. For more than a minute, while Armstrong stood staring after her dumbly, she remained so; her face pressed against the cold pane, looking out upon the white earth. Deliberately, normally, she turned.

Seemingly without an effort, so naturally that even Armstrong was deceived, she smiled.

"Pardon me," she said evenly. "I'm not often hysterical." She was returning slowly. "I'll be glad when vacation comes. I think I'm— tired." She seated herself and motioned the other back into his place,—a motion that was a command. "Now, tell me, please, that you didn't mean what you said a moment ago when we were both irresponsible. It will make us both sleep better."

The smile had left Armstrong's face now, and in its place was the pallor of reaction. But he was quiet also.

"I wish I could," he said steadily, "but I can't. It'll be exactly as it was before."

The girl was still smiling,—that same normal, apparently effortless, smile.

"Nonsense!" she refuted, in tones deliberately matter-of-fact. "There's all the difference in the world. Before you had no audience. And now—the entire country will listen now."

"It doesn't matter," dully. "It's always been you that counted really. Success was an incident, but you were the real incentive."

"I?" She laughed gently. "On the contrary it was I who tried to lead you away from your work, to make you practical. Don't you remember the Graham offer?"

"Yes," hurriedly. "I've thought of it a thousand times. It was the big mistake of my life when I refused his proposal. If I'd accepted then—"

"You'd not have been a successful writer whose work goes on sale to-day in every city in the United States."

"Perhaps. But I would have had you. What do I care for success in comparison to you!"

Listening, just for an instant the girl's nostrils tightened; again she laughed.

"We seem to be travelling in a circle," she bantered, "and keep returning to the starting-point. It's discouraging."

"It's written," said Armstrong, simply. "We can't avoid it. With me you're the starting-point as you're the end, always. Didn't you recognize yourself so in the last novel?"

The girl settled back in her seat wearily.

"You told me, I recall," she said.

"And in the one before?"

"You told me that also."

Armstrong was observing her steadily.

"You are in the new one too," he said; "the one I've been working on—but which will never be completed now. You've killed the girl there too, Elice."

"Steve!" The hands had gone swiftly to the girl's ears, covered them completely. "I shan't listen. This is worse than folly. It's madness."

"I can't help it," monotonously. "It's myself. I can't avoid being myself."

"Nor I myself, Steve," very gently. "Can't you realize that?"

The man passed his hand across his eyes as though brushing away something tangible.

"No, I can't realize anything," he said dully, "except that I love you—and have lost. This and that the world is dead—and I am alone in it."

For the second time the girl arose, and even yet quite steadily. But at last her lips were trembling.

"I think you had better go now," she requested. "I can't stand this much longer; and besides, to keep it up would do no good that I can see. To-morrow is Saturday, and if you still feel there is anything you must say to me I shall be at home all day. But to-night—please go now."

As in a dream, Armstrong arose, obeying her command—as he always obeyed in small things.

"Yes, I suppose you're right," he echoed dully. "I realize I'm only making matters worse by staying, only getting us farther apart." He buttoned his coat to the chin and drew on his gloves lingeringly. "If I were to call to-morrow, though, isn't there a chance that you would be different? Can't I have even—hope?"

The girl said nothing, did not appear to hear. Subconsciously she was counting the seconds, almost with prayer; counting until she should be alone.

But still Armstrong dallied, killing those same seconds wilfully.

"Aren't you going to offer me even hope, Elice?" he repeated. "I'll be in—hell when I go, without even hope."

It was the final straw, that prophetic suggestion, the snapping straw. With one gesture of hopeless, impotent misery, of infinite appeal as well, the girl threw out her hand.

"Go," she pleaded brokenly, "go quickly. There's a limit to everything and with me that limit is reached." She motioned again, and Steve went out into the night.

CHAPTER IX

ADMONITION

There was a light in the den as Darley Roberts, having let himself in with his latch-key, started up the stairs toward his own rooms, and, although he moved softly, Harry Randall himself faced the newcomer on the landing, his hand extended.

"I was waiting for you," he announced without preface. "I felt sure you'd be in to-night sometime." He was smiling a welcome, one unmistakably genuine. "Delayed, were you?"

"Yes. A wreck out about seventy miles. I just got in on the relief," laconically. The accompanying grip, however, was not curt. "You'll read about it in the morning. Looks comfortable in there," with a nod toward the inviting den. "Early enough yet for a chat, is it?"

"I was hoping so. That's why I sat up."

"Thanks. I'll be with you in a minute."

Shortly, in lounging-robe and slippers this time, he came tiptoeing down the hall past the other sleeping-rooms; a big alert shape that seemed mountainous beside the lesser Randall idly awaiting his return.

"Very well," he introduced characteristically as he dropped into a convenient seat, "let's hear all about it—everything. I'm listening."

Randall caught the contagion of brevity, as he always did when in the other's presence. "What would you like to hear about first?" he returned smilingly. "Have you any choice?"

"Yourself," with a steady look. "Everything's right, I see."

"Yes, everything's right," echoed Randall, "so much so that I'm simply foolishly happy." He paused meaningly. "And now, since—"

Roberts gestured—merely gestured.

"Aren't you going to permit me even to thank you?" countered Randall.

"I came to hear the news," evenly. Roberts smiled suddenly at the look on his companion's face. "I understand about that other matter," he digressed, ambiguously but nevertheless adequately; "let it go at that. Mrs. Randall, I presume—"

"She hung your portrait, life size, in the parlor downstairs a few days ago," with direct malice.

Again Roberts gestured; then he looked up. They laughed together and the tabooed subject by mutual consent passed into oblivion.

"Miss Gleason—Elice—" suggested Roberts.

"Still at her place in the university." Randall busied himself with a strand of lint on the collar of his smoking-jacket. "Her father's gone all to pieces, you know, and she seems a bit—tired. Otherwise she's herself—as always."

"No, I didn't know," said Roberts. "And Armstrong?"

"He's been working steadily for months, and been straight absolutely." Randall ventured a glance at last. "To-day was his big day; you do know that. He was in the clouds this evening."

"I should like to have been with you." The tone was non-committal. "Strange to say I like to see people in that frame of mind. It makes for optimism. Will his new effort, you think, stand on its own legs?"

"Yes; always providing nothing interferes. I've seen the first half. It's more than good. It's excellent. You're in it, distinct as life, by the way."

Roberts lit a cigar and smoked for a minute in silence.

"I'm sorry, sincerely, that I'm there," he said then. He gazed at his companion steadily, and with a significance Randall never forgot. "I used to fancy I wasn't afraid of anything. I'm not afraid of most things,—dynamite or nitro-glycerine or murderous fanatics or physical pain; but in the last year I've learned there's one thing on earth, one person, I'm afraid of—deathly afraid. You know who?"

"Yes."

"I predicted once he would make good. I believed it then. Since I've been alone a good deal and had much time to think, and question. That's why I am afraid." Roberts paused to smoke, seemingly impassive. "I'd give every cent I have in the world and start anew to-morrow without breakfast if I could only know, only know to a certainty that he would keep his grip. But will he?... I'm afraid!"

Scarcely knowing what he did, Randall lit a cigar in turn and smoked like a furnace. His tongue attempted to form an assurance, but try as he might he could not give it voice. Once he had promised not to lie to that man opposite, ever; and in the depths of his own soul he knew that he, too, was afraid. At last, in self-confessed rout, he voiced the commonplace.

"It's my turn to ask questions now, I think," he said. "Are you back to stay?"

Roberts looked up, only half comprehending; he roused himself.

"No. I intend to close out everything. I doubt if I ever stay anywhere permanently again. I'll keep the house here, though."

"You've decided not to sell it—even to me?"

Roberts paused.

"Yes," he said at last; but he offered no explanation.

Randall waited, hoping for a lead whereby light might come. But none opened, and the subject dropped.

"I judge the mine's making good," he commented, with the trace of awkwardness he always felt when approaching the other's personal affairs. "Will you return soon?"

"Probably not soon." The voice was almost listless. "I put everything in shape for an indefinite absence before I came away. To answer your question: It's a wonder, bigger than I ever hoped. It'll still be a great mine a generation from now."

Randall caught his breath. The big game was yet new to him, and the volume of wealth suggested was cumulatively overpowering.

"Bigger than you expected!" he echoed. "Then that means — millions!"

Roberts glanced at his companion curiously. Slowly he smiled.

"Yes," he said, "it means millions. I haven't even an idea how many eventually." The smile left his face, every trace of expression as well. "I could sell for ten to-day if I wished; but I have no intention of selling."

Randall sat looking at the other as if hypnotized. He forgot to ask questions, forgot almost to breathe. To read of gigantic fortunes, the property of absolute strangers living a thousand or thousands of miles away, is one thing: to have one personally known, an actual acquaintance in possession — it held him speechless, staring. The other's familiar, tolerant laugh aroused him.

"Don't, please," said Roberts. "They've been doing that to me wherever I show myself and write my name; that is, when they haven't been proving relationship." He laughed again shortly. "It's wonderful how many relatives I've discovered of late and friends I've made. Don't do it, please."

Randall could still color and his face went red.

"I beg your pardon," he apologized, "I — "

"Nor that either," swiftly, almost curtly. "Just be yourself, natural. I like you that way." He looked at the other openly, with frank intentness that heralded the unexpected.

"It's possible," he digressed evenly, "that I'll be here some time, but the chances are I'll only stay a day or so. After to-night we'll probably not see much of each other, maybe nothing at all, ever. We're rather different types and our roads lead differently." He smiled to dissipate the mystification he saw gathering on the other's face. "This is a preface. What I'm aiming at directly is to say a thing or two that have been on my mind for some time—in case I don't have the opportunity again." Once more the smile,—the same smile that had won the confidence of the other against heavy odds in the beginning of their acquaintance. "Do you mind if I'm a bit—fatherly to you?"

"No." Swift as thought, as panoramic memory, Harry Randall had remembered everything; and, without shame, his eyes were moist. "I'd like you to be so. I understand."

Roberts looked away at the red and green wall opposite.

"It's just this, then; and if you wish me to stop say the word; I get reports of various things in various ways. It's part of my philosophy to know of events in advance if I can. I've heard that you are speculating a bit. Is it true?"

Randall started involuntarily; but the other was not looking.

"How in the world did you know?" he questioned.

"Never mind how I know. I'd tell you if it would do any good; but it wouldn't. It's true, isn't it?"

"Yes," Randall moistened his lips; "a little."

"Things coming a trifle slow for you, are they? Hard to meet expenses—"

"No; it's not that; but—"

"I understand perfectly." Roberts was still inspecting the pattern of the paper with minute attention. "As perhaps your best friend, though, don't do it. If at any time you need money, really need it, remember I am your friend, and don't hesitate to tell me. But outside of that—" He halted significantly, waiting; then, sufficient time having elapsed, he looked at the other again directly.

"Now for the fatherly admonition," he digressed evenly, "or whatever you please to call it. You're doing well here, and will do better as time goes by. You're on your own feet, solid. Don't gamble with things as they are, ever. It's contagious, I know, when a man gets a little surplus, and looking over the rise of the horizon sees such an infinite field beyond; but steer clear. Some men can gamble and lose, and forget it and come up smiling again. Others are fashioned by nature differently. Once down they stay down; and regret as long as they live. It's a fundamental difference no power can change. I hope I haven't hurt you unforgivably, Randall?"

Harry Randall glanced up, and his eyes held steady.

"No; and I'll not forget. I promise you that." Involuntarily he started to rise, his hand half extended, his eyes bright; but he sat down again. "If I could only thank you right, Roberts," he voiced tensely, "could only show you in some way that I appreciate—" He halted, the sentence so consciously inadequate, incomplete,—"If I only could," he repeated helplessly.

A moment they sat there so, looking at each other, merely looking. Then at last, with an obvious weariness Randall had never seen him exhibit before, Roberts slowly arose. Still another moment he stood there, looking down.

"'Roberts,'" he echoed in a low tone, "'Roberts,' always 'Roberts'! Not 'Darley,' even then." He turned abruptly toward his own rooms, his great shoulders all but blocking the doorway as he passed out. "Good-night," he said.

CHAPTER X

DECISION

The light on the porch was dim, and as Elice Gleason, answering the ring, opened the outer door she stared as one who sees unbelievable things. For a moment she did not utter a sound, merely stood there gazing at the visitor with a look that was only partially credulous; in sudden weakness, oddly unlike her normal composure, she covered her face with her hands.

"Elice!" Unbidden, the man came wholly within. "A thousand pardons for startling you. I should have let you know—'phoned at least. I—pardon me, please."

With an effort the girl removed her hands, but Darley Roberts saw she was still trembling.

"No need to apologize." She closed the door mechanically. "You did surprise me, it's true; but that wasn't the trouble really. I've been expecting something to happen all day, something that hasn't happened yet, and when you rang I fancied—" She laughed, as though the inadequate explanation were complete and withal a thing of trivial moment. "You remember once I told you I believed, after all, you had nerves. I'm making the tardy discovery that I've got them myself."

In his turn Roberts smiled and ignored the obvious. He seldom anticipated, this man.

"Yes, we all have them, I guess," he dismissed, "along with an appendix and a few other superfluous items." He was still standing just within the doorway. "First of all, though, I don't intrude? Harry Randall told me about your father."

"He's been much better to-day, and he's asleep this evening already." In swift reaction the girl was herself again, more than her recent self, positively gay. "Intrude!" she laughed softly. "You're actually becoming humorous; and as you would say, your dearest enemies have never accused you of that before. Come."

Between genteel poverty and absolute poverty there are distinguishing signs and Darley Roberts observed all things; but not once from his point of vantage in the den he recalled so well did he seem to take observations—any more than he seemed to see the alteration, likewise unmistakable, in the girl herself.

"It seems as though it were only yesterday instead of—I don't like to think how many ages ago, I was here last," he commented as he relaxed in familiar comfort. "If you just had one of those linen things you used to work on, and—"

The ball of white, like a crumpled handkerchief, which had been lying idle in the girl's lap was unrolled and, before the speaker's eyes, there appeared against the colorless background a clover with four leaves.

"Elice!" It was unfeigned surprise. "Is this another regiment or are you still working on that last one yet?"

The girl sorted her silks in demure impassivity.

"Another regiment entirely—or is it an army? I've forgotten how many comprise a regiment." She went to work with steady fingers. "These lunch cloths of mine are becoming as staple as soap or quinine."

Roberts watched as the needle went through and through, but he did not smile. He could not.

"Another regiment! Then I haven't really been sleeping," he said. "For a moment when that four-leafed clover showed—By the way, do you happen to recall what day of the month this is?"

"Yes." The girl's eyes did not leave her work. "I remembered it the first thing when I got up this morning."

"You remembered? And still you were surprised when I came. Didn't you think I'd remember too?"

"I didn't doubt it."

"And come to commemorate the date, December the sixth?"

"Commemorate, yes. Come? I didn't know. I hoped—until it grew dark; then—one loses certainty alone after dark."

"It wasn't that which you had expected all day to happen, though," said Roberts, evenly.

The girl did not dissimulate.

"No," she said simply.

One step nearer had they approached the mystery, one step only, but the man came no further—then.

"And weren't you going to commemorate it yourself, since you remembered?" he digressed.

"Yes, I have done so. I've been celebrating all day. I haven't washed a dish; they're all stacked out in the kitchen. And this—" she stood up deliberately and turned about that the other might see—"is my party gown, worn in honor of the occasion." She returned to her place and again the needle passed methodically in and out of the linen. "Are you satisfied?"

"Satisfied!" It was the rebellious cry of a dominant thing trapped and suffering. "Satisfied!" By pure force of will he held back the flood. "Elice, won't you please put up that work—for to-night? It's—ghastly."

As though paralyzed, the white hands paused, for half a minute lay idle. Without comment she obeyed.

"You know what I mean," said the man. "It makes me irresponsible. I want to throttle the something somewhere to blame."

"I'm sorry. I didn't mean to hurt you. If I had expected for an instant—"

"Don't, please!" It was supplication from one accustomed to command. "Talk about human beings being pawns in the game or straws before the whirlwind!" Again the curt repression by pure force of will, and the inevitable pause with the digression complete following. "I haven't heard your report of yourself yet, Elice. It's due me, overdue. I promised you not to write, and kept my word, you know."

The girl looked at him with eyes that tried to smile.

"Ask me anything else and I'll answer," she said. "This I can't answer, because there's nothing to be said. I've merely been waiting."

"As you were to-night, when I startled you?"

The girl's lips tightened, but they relaxed. She was in command now.

"Yes," she said.

It was the second step; and for the second time the man approached no nearer—then.

"Won't you let me ask you questions instead," countered the girl, "as a favor?"

"Certainly, if you prefer."

"'If I prefer.'" She mouthed the words deliberately. "Very well, then. What have you been doing since I saw you last?"

Roberts gave her an odd look.

"Getting older mostly," he said.

"I might have chronicled that fact myself," echoed the girl.

"Very fast," added the man, evenly. "Did you notice my hair?"

"It is grayer—a bit," reluctantly.

"Grayer!" Roberts laughed. "I made a microscopical examination recently for one hair of the original color to preserve as a relic. It was too late. Do you care to volunteer in the search?"

The girl ignored the invitation.

"What else did you do?" she asked.

"Worked some." Roberts held up his great hands, calloused heavily over the palms. "I've learned several things by actual experience: drilling, dynamiting, sharpening steel, mucking ore, assaying — everything."

"And what else?" relentlessly.

"Prospected a little. Ran out of provisions and went two days without a bite to eat. Returned to find a strike on at the mine — and the strikers in possession." He halted reminiscently. "I knocked a man down that day: the leader. He dared me and there were a dozen others backing him up. It was him or me and it couldn't be avoided. In the affair I hurt my hand; while it was healing I went to 'Frisco and took in the theatres." He held up the member indicated, reversed this time for inspection. A white jagged scar ran diagonally over the knuckles. "It's entirely well now."

The girl caught her breath. No query this time.

The hand returned idly to the man's lap. He looked away.

"It's a rough life out there," he resumed evenly, "wild and primitive; but it's fascinating in a way. Besides, it's one of the things I wanted to know. I think I do know it. I don't believe any one could fool me on a mine now."

Elice Gleason looked at him steadily, until perforce he returned her gaze.

"Granted," she admitted steadily; "but is it worth while?"

"Worth while? How do I know — or any one. It's necessary for some one to know. It's part of the big game. Farther than that — My hair is all gray now — and I don't know."

His companion looked away, with a little gesture of impatience.

"Last of all, the mine itself?" she suggested.

Roberts hesitated, his face inscrutable as a book closed.

"If I knew what you wanted to know," he said at last, "I'd tell you; but I don't. It's fabulous, if that answers your question. It's like Aladdin's lamp: there's nothing material on the face of the earth it won't give for the asking. It's producing enough now daily to keep a sane man a year. It's power infinite for good or evil, and creating more power day by day." He halted, then unconsciously repeated himself. "Yes, power infinite, neither more nor less."

There was a long silence before his companion spoke.

"And power, you said once, was the thing you wanted most. You have it at last."

"Yes, I have it at last, that's true. I can command the services of a thousand men, to work for me or amuse me; or for another if I direct. I can pass current anywhere at any time, and make any one I care to name pass current with me. The master key is in my possession tight. I can choose my tools for whatever I wish done from a multitude. The material is limitless, for I can pay. Besides, as I said before, this power is increasing inevitably, whether I'm asleep or awake, growing by its own momentum. I have it at last, yes; but it neither is nor ever was what I wanted most, Elice. I said I wanted it, you're right; but I never said I wanted it most. You know what I want most in the world, Elice."

Listening, Elice Gleason folded her hands tight, until the blood left the fingers.

"Yes, I know," she said steadily. "We understand each other; it's useless to pretend otherwise. I've tried, and you've seen through the disguise and smiled. It's simply useless." The clasped hands opened in a gesture of dismissal. "But don't let's speak of it now. I want to hear your plans for the future. What are you going to do now that you have—power?"

"Do?" Roberts looked at her steadily. "That depends upon one condition absolutely. It's superfluous for me to name that one."

The girl flashed him a look from eyes unnaturally bright.

"Please," she pleaded, "leave it alone for a time. You have two courses outlined, an option. It would be unlike you otherwise. What are those two?"

"I didn't mean to be insistent, Elice," said Roberts, gently. "Take my word for it, I shan't be again, whatever you decide. Yes; I see two ways ahead. In one, work will be secondary, another's happiness first, always first. In the other, I shall work—to forget. The incentive of the game itself is gone. I've won the game. But there is no other way to forget and retain self-respect; so I shall work—to the end."

"And you must decide soon?"

"Yes, at once. I can't remain longer in uncertainty. Nothing is so bad as that. It's like a bungling execution: infinitely better for all concerned to be complete. To-morrow I take up the trail one way or the other."

Opposite, the girl caught her breath for an instant; but though the other saw he said nothing. He had promised he would not.

"You'll leave then to-morrow, if—" That was all.

"Yes."

"And never come back, never?"

"Not unless I am sent for. Life is short and holds enough pain at best. I have several projects in mind, and I shall be free to follow them where they lead. I'll go to Mexico first. They've barely scratched the resources down there. Later I go to South America. Afterward—I haven't planned. I'll simply follow the lead. There's work enough to do."

The girl looked at him—through eyes that held their old marvel, almost their old fear.

"You can cut yourself off so, from all the old life, really?" she voiced.

"Yes, Elice."

It was finality absolute, the last word, the ultimatum.

"And still you love me?" breathed the girl low.

"More than I love life. You don't doubt it."

From her seat the girl arose abruptly and passed the length of the room with long, unconscious strides, like a man. She made no effort at dissimulation or concealment now. The time for that was past. She merely fought—openly, but in silence. Once she sat down for a moment; but for a moment only. Again she was on her feet. A bit later she asked the time, and very quietly Roberts told her. She went to the window in the front of the house commanding the street and scrutinized its length. She returned and resumed her seat.

"Can I help you in any way, Elice?" asked Roberts, gently.

The girl shook her head.

"No," she said steadily. "No one can help me. I can't even help myself. That's the curse of it. There's nothing to do but wait." The folded hands changed position one above the other, and after a moment returned as before. "Do you understand?" she queried without preface.

An instant Roberts hesitated, but an instant only.

"Yes, I think so. You intimated you were expecting some one to come."

"Something to happen," substituted the girl.

"It's all the same," evenly.

Silence followed for a space while they sat there so; breaking it, the girl looked at the other directly.

"I have refused him definitely," she said, without consciousness of the seeming ambiguity of the remark. "I did so last night."

"Yes," very low; and that was all.

The girl drew a long breath, like one preparing for the unknown.

"I could see no other way of finding out for sure. Like yourself, nothing seemed to me so bad as uncertainty."

"Yes," once more; just "yes."

"He sat just where you are sitting now; and when I told him he laughed." A second the brown eyes dropped, then in infinite pathos they returned to the listener's face. "You know how he laughs when he's irresponsible. It was horrible."

"I know," echoed Roberts. "I've heard it."

"And then he went away. I sent him away. I couldn't stand any more then. It seemed to me I'd go mad if I tried."

Although the room was warm, the girl was shivering; rising, Roberts lit the gas in the grate. But he said nothing, absolutely nothing.

Through wide-open eyes the girl watched him as he returned to his seat. Involuntarily she threw out both arms in a gesture of impotency absolute.

"That's all," she completed, "except that I told him to return—if he felt he must. I've been expecting him every minute all day; anticipating horrors. But I haven't heard a word."

It was the mystery at last, impersonate. Like a live presence it stood there between these two human beings in the room, holding them apart, and each in his separate place.

Not for a moment but for minutes this time they sat in silence. Neither thought of speaking commonplaces now, nor again of things intimate. The period for these was past; the present too compellingly vital. What the man was thinking he did not say nor reveal by so much as an expression. He had given his word not to do so; and with Darley Roberts a promise was sacred. A question he did ask, though, at last.

"Wouldn't you like me to go and find out for certain, Elice?" he suggested. "I'll do so if you wish."

"No." It was almost a plea. "We'll find out soon, very soon, I'm positive. I'll know whatever he does. He's certain to tell me; and I wish you here if he comes. Besides, neither of us could do anything whatever to alter the inevitable, even if we tried. We must simply wait; it can't be much longer now."

Once more there was a long silence, ghastly in its dragging moments, and again broken by the man.

"I shan't trouble you to go through the argument again, Elice," he said, "or attempt to alter your decision, whatever it may be. I can't presume to judge another's soul. But, merely to know for certain: you've decided positively to marry him, if—" The sentence ended in silence and a gesture.

His companion did not answer, appeared almost not to hear.

"Tell me, please," repeated the man gently. "You may as well. It won't hurt either of us any more for you to say it—if you've so decided."

"Yes," answered the girl this time. "I've tried and tried to find an escape; but there is none." She passed her hand over her throat as though the words choked her, but her voice was now steady. "His blood would be upon my head, always, if I could prevent and still let him go—down. God help you and me both, but I can't do otherwise!"

A moment longer Roberts sat still—fixedly still; he stood up, his great hands clenched until they were as white as the scar itself.

"I think I'd better go now," he said, "before Armstrong comes." The great shoulders of him were swelling and receding visibly with each breath. "I don't know, of course; but I fear to go passive and unresisting to the stake myself, and to remain passive and unresisting when I saw the same fire that was to be my fate touching you, scorching you slowly to death—and for a fault that was neither of your making nor mine, for which we are in no respect responsible—I'm afraid that is beyond me, Elice. I'd better go at once, before he comes."

"No." The girl, too, was on her feet facing him. "Please don't. You don't really mean what you just said."

"Don't I? You believe in miracles. I'm human and I'd throttle him if he came while I was here—and came as he came once before!"

"Stop! in pity. If it does happen he'll not be to blame; it will be because he can't help it. You're big and strong and he'll need you as well as me. Wait."

The man drew back a step, but his great jaw was set immovably.

"You can't realize what you're asking," he said. "Remember my conviction is not your conviction. I still believe that two predominate over one and that nature's law comes first. I'll go because it is your decision and final; but I can't change elemental things at command. Don't ask it or expect it, because it is impossible."

"It's not impossible, though," desperately. "Nothing is impossible with you."

Roberts' great head shook a negative.

"This is. I can't discuss it longer. Good-bye, Elice."

The girl's brown eyes followed him as, decisively now, he prepared to leave, and in hopeless, abject misery. She spoke one word.

"Darley," she said.

The listener halted, motionless as a figure in clay.

"Darley," repeated the girl; and again that was all.

"'Darley!'" It was the man's voice this time, but it sounded as though coming from a distance. "'Darley!' At last!—and now!"

"Darley," yet once again, "as I love you and you love me don't—desert me now!"

On the room fell a silence like death,—to those two actors worse than death; for it held thought infinite and complete realization at last of what might have been and was not; of what as well, unless a miracle intervened, could never be. In it they stood, each where he was, two figures in clay instead of one. Interrupting, awakening, torturing, sounded the thing they had so long expected; the impact of a step upon the floor of the porch without; a moment later another, uncertain, and another; a pause, and then, startlingly loud, the trill of an electric bell.

For an instant neither stirred. It was the expected; and still there is a limit to human endurance. The girl was trembling, in a nervous tension too great to bear longer. An effort indeed she made at control; but it was a pitiful effort and futile. In surrender absolute, abandon absolute, she dropped back into her seat, her arms crossed pathetically on the surface of the library table, her face buried from sight therein.

"Answer it, please," she pleaded. "I can't. I'm ashamed, unutterably; but I can't!"

Again the alarm of the bell sounded; curtly short this time and insistent.

Without a word or even a pause Darley Roberts obeyed. As he passed out he closed the door carefully behind him.

Five minutes that seemed to the girl a lifetime dragged by. Listening, she heard the opening of the front door, the murmur of low, speaking voices,—a murmur ceasing as abruptly as it began; then, wonder of wonders, the door closed again with a snap and a retreating step sounded once, twice, as when it had come, on the floor of the porch. Following, she marked the even footfall of Roberts returning. The electric switch that he had turned on snapped back as he had found it, the intervening door opened, and he entered. But, strange to say, he did not pause or say a word. As one awakening from a dream and not yet wholly conscious, he returned silently to his former place. On his face was a look she had never seen before, which she could not fathom.

"Darley." Unbelieving the girl leaned toward him appealingly. "Tell me. Wasn't it—he?"

The man looked at her then, and there was that in his gray eyes that tinged her face crimson.

"No. It was Harry Randall," he said. "It's all right, Elice. The miracle came."

"The miracle!" The voice was uncertain again, but from a far different cause this time. "Don't keep me waiting. Tell me. Is he—well?"

This time Roberts actually smiled,—smiled as he had not done before in months.

"Yes; and writing like mad! That's the miracle. He's been at it steady now for twenty hours, and won't even pause to eat. He sent for Harry to deliver the message. It's inspiration he's working under and he couldn't stop to come himself, wouldn't. He said to tell you, and me, that it was all right. He'd found himself at last. Those were his words,—he'd found himself at last." As suddenly as it had come the smile passed, and Roberts stood up, his big hands locked behind his back.

"We've thought we understood him all these years," he said steadily, "but at last I realize that we haven't at all. It would be humorous if it hadn't been so near to tragedy, so very near. Anyway, it's clear now. Harry Randall sees it too. That's why he wouldn't stay. Steve Armstrong never cared for you really at all, Elice. He thought he did—but he didn't. It was himself he cared for; and a fancy. Neither you nor I nor any one can change him or help him more than temporarily. We're free. He'll stand or go under as it was written in the beginning." The voice lowered until it throbbed with the conviction that was in the speaker's soul. "No man alive who really cared could find inspiration where he found it. The world is before us and we're free, Elice, free!"

Unconsciously, in answer to an instinct she obeyed without reason, the girl too arose, an exaltation in her face no artist could reproduce nor words describe.

"Yes," she said. "I see it all too at last. We've all been blind." She caught her breath at the thought that would intrude, force it back as she would. "And still we came so near, so very, very near —"

"Yes; but it's past." The man opposite was advancing. Not the impassive, cold Darley Roberts the world knew, but the other Darley Roberts revealed to one alone; the isolate human alone and lonely. "But it's past, past, do you hear? And to-day is December the sixth, our anniversary — ours." He halted, waiting. He smiled, with a tenderness infinite. "Is it 'Darley' still, Elice? Won't you come and say it again?"

THE END

CPSIA information can be obtained
at www.ICGtesting.com
Printed in the USA
LVHW031240080121
675759LV00004B/265